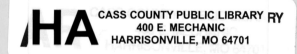

Sea Gift

BY

JOHN ASHBY

Clarion Books

For Cathy

I would like to thank my family and friends for their support and care. I would also like to thank Robin Straus for her advice and for taking a chance on presenting this book, and to offer very special thanks to Jennifer Greene for her patient and diligent edits and insights.

Clarion Books
a Houghton Mifflin Company imprint
215 Park Avenue South, New York, NY 10003
Copyright © 2003 by John Ashby

The text was set in 12-point Dutch 766 BT.

www.houghtonmifflinbooks.com

Printed in the U.S.A.

Library of Congress Cataloging-in-Publication Data

Ashby, John.
Sea gift / by John Ashby.
p. cm.
Summary: While working on the lobster boats in his Nova Scotia town, thirteen-year-old Lauchie hauls up an old crock that hides a letter that sends him on a quest for treasure that was hidden long ago.
ISBN 0-395-77603-1
[1. Buried treasure—Fiction. 2. Lobster fishers—Fiction. 3. Nova Scotia—Fiction.] I. Title.
PZ7.A814Se 2003
[Fic]—dc21
2003002476

MP 10 9 8 7 6 5 4 3 2 1

Contents

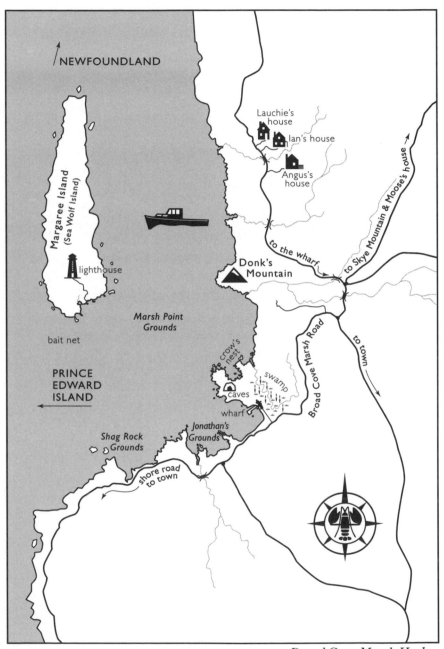

Broad Cove Marsh Harbor

Author's Note

Broad Cove Marsh Harbor is a real place, a tiny harbor much like my description, and the little bay called the Crow's Nest is a good place for a few big market lobsters after the water warms up. The place names and grounds are also real; I could never have thought of better. The people are totally fictional—a conglomerate of the influences of many.

The area is a Scots community on the northwestern shore of Cape Breton Island, Nova Scotia, which forms the southern arm of the Gulf of St. Lawrence.

Angus, Lauchie (pronounced *Lawkee*), Rodie, and Danny are some very popular first names, and as a consequence first names are often doubled to avoid confusion. Dan Angus is not Angus, Dan, or Danny; and Rodie Jim differs from Rodie, Jim, RJ, and even Jim Rodie. This may seem strange to some, but it is part of the voice of the land. You will probably notice that I wisely avoid any surnames whatsoever.

For the needs of the story, I made the lobster season later than it is because I didn't want Lauchie and Angus to skip school. The kind of storm they run into on first day would be less likely so late in the season.

The dangerous rock is still there, but well clear of the wharf, and not very dangerous at all. The caves? "Ah, well, they're all blocked off now."

1

GOALS

In a momentary lull in the driving snow, the moon broke through low, scudding clouds, revealing the first outrider of the season's pack ice, a glowing silver finger six miles long and as far away, seeming to hover a quarter off the bow. It appeared deceptively still, its ethereal beauty emphasized by the brevity of its revelation, as the thirty-knot wind that drove it obliterated the scene in another swirling snow squall.

The dream always began this way. Trapped in the strange logic of nightmares, Lauchie both felt the rolling deck of the big fishing boat and saw it from afar. He both watched the dream and was the dream. He was a grown man of the past in the night-wracked mind of a boy.

The dragger slid down a great long wave, then seemed to balk in the trough. He felt the hesitation, but his first thought was for the boat, not the net astern her. The engine's pitch deepened. The dragger seemed to shudder; then, with a lurch, she rose into the long back slope of the wave. It was a tiny pause, an instant's warning followed by an instant's relief, then the realization of the loss of load and the easier sound of the big diesel.

If the cable had broken long and deep, the resistant sea might have tamed it. It broke short.

The cable sprang from the water like a waiting predator, one hundred feet of writhing, twisted steel released from the strain of an eight-ton pull; its keening passage muted by the din of engine, wind, and sea; its searching coils shrouded in gusting snow.

He sensed danger the instant before it struck, driving the numb, salty taste of heavy shock to the back of his nose. He was hurled from the deck, slapped into the face of the wave, driven deep into its icy core. The air exploded from his shattered chest. He gasped and took in seawater several degrees below freezing.

The body slowly drifted in silence to the bottom of the cold, dark sea. As always, even in the throes of the nightmare, Lauchie felt guilt-shrouded relief. It wasn't him—it was his father.

Lauchie awoke shaking. He turned his alarm off and pulled his covers tighter, wondering how the dream knew when to start so that it would always end with the alarm. He grasped at the reality of the new day, thinking of the game that coming night. They would be playing on home ice against the team from the Micmac community, thirty miles away. Lauchie imagined scoring a goal, visualized every move until he could see the puck slamming into the net. To score he'd have to get around Moose, the big Indian defenseman, bigger than most adults and a lot bigger than Lauchie.

Feeling better, he let himself recognize the dream. His mom knew about it, but he could never share the details with her. He felt embarrassed because it was so real, yet he had no way to verify the facts. They came either from forgotten phrases that he'd overheard when neighbors thought he wasn't there, or simply from his imagination. It felt like an infringement, as though he were witnessing something that he shouldn't. People said he looked like his dad, but he had no living image of his father, only faded, still, frozen photographs. Lauchie cherished those pictures but couldn't imagine his thirteen-year-old face becoming one of those images that grinned back at him from old trucks and unfamiliar decks. He could never explain these things. Even stranger would be explaining that he also cherished the dream. It was his. "Must be crazy," he muttered in perplexity. People said his dad had a wicked wit, that he was a fine boatman, a good fisherman who had loved the sea. "Me, too," Lauchie murmured to himself. "I'm gonnah be a fisherman . . . with my own boat. The dream is just a sometimes thing of the night."

Lauchie's thoughts were interrupted by his mom's voice from downstairs. "Are you up yet? It's getting late."

"Yah, yah, I'm comin'."

Lauchie's odds looked bad. The puck was just off the boards and up ice from his goal. He was closest and coming in fast. Moose was at an angle in front of him. Lauchie could see that he, the Moose, and the puck were all going to come together. He'd be a smear on the boards. In a flash of insight spurred by desperation, Lauchie saw the pattern. He sensed Angus coming in from center, stood hard on his edges, and stretched for the puck. He was so extended that he needed the leverage of the boards to flick a weak pass to Angus. Then he snapped back his stick and headed up ice. Moose was overcommitted, coming in like a freight train. The puck skittered past him. Too late, the big defenseman half-corrected, lost it, and smashed face-on into the boards.

The ice was wide open. Lauchie charged up the ice with the choppy stroke of a short skater. He heard the quiet snap of Angus's pass, risked a quick glance, and saw that he'd have to reach for it.

He made the stretch, capturing the puck with a satisfying *thwack*, scooted it ahead, and wound up for a slap shot that was not to be. He flipped the puck to his left as he arced across the goal mouth, flicking it back again to the right at the last second, then leaned back and shot it into the right corner as he swept past the post.

The puck wobbled in a soft lift. The goalie went down, his leg stretching, stretching, his gloved stick-hand moving to close the gap. The puck cleared the big glove in a tumbling flight that seemed to float into the netting.

Lauchie concentrated on making a perfect, casual, glancing-back circle in the corner. He rested on his stick, which lay across his knees and coasted to his right wing position. The hidden grin directed down at the ice almost hurt his face.

Lauchie heard Uncle Ian shout, "Pretty goal!" He heard Dan Angus's voice, sounding like it wasn't raised at all, drifting through the murmur of the stands: "Go Lauchie!" He stared at the ice, still resting on his stick. When he had his grin under control, his look nonchalant, he glanced up toward Ian and Dan Angus and gave the nod, pulling his chin down just a bit to the left, the way Dan Angus did. He looked over at Angus; gave him a flat-eyed nod with a quick double gum chew. The puck was being dropped. There were still ten minutes of play.

When they came out, snow was blowing in horizontal sheets. It felt good on Lauchie's face, still hot from indoors, and melted, glistening, on his curly red hair. The air smelled tangy with fresh snow, and the sizzling sound of its drifting filled the gaps between moaning gusts. Lights from the arena and from pickup trucks blended in a yellow glow, friendly and exciting in the surrounding blackness.

The driver sat in the big idling highway plow, his arm resting on the open window; the blue roof light strobed through the driving snow. He was hollering, unaware how loudly his voice carried over the engine sound. "I'm makin' my last run down the shore road . . . blowin' too hard . . . callin' in the plows . . . be no school tomorrow."

The players' rides set off in a cavalcade, following one another's taillights behind the plow. Lauchie and Angus sat scrunched between Dan Angus, who was driving, and Ian. The slap of the windshield wipers was hypnotic and comforting. Gusts of wind rocked the truck, briefly whiting out the cones of light and matting the windshield with darkening snow, emphasizing the warmth of the cab.

"Nice play you boys made," Dan Angus said, as he switched on the marine band.

The voice on the radio was familiar. "Strait of Northumberland, Magdalene Islands, Cape Breton shores, and Georges Banks: Freezing-spray warning is in effect, northwesterly winds eighteen knots, gusting to twenty-four, blowing snow, visibility zero."

Dan Angus turned it off. "Can see that," he muttered. "They're sayin' all of Nova Scotia's snowed in."

"What a goal," Angus said, giving Lauchie a jab. "You sure suckered that big dumb Indian."

"It was a good play," Ian remarked, "because that big kid is one of the best players I've ever seen on our ice. I'd be proud to beat him. I'd not call him dumb."

"Well, we scored—not him," Angus said, laughing.

"Yah," Lauchie agreed.

"I don't understand you kids," Ian said. "It's a hockey game. Is he the enemy or what?"

"Yah," Angus said. "He's different, not from round here."

"We're the good guys, they're the bad guys," Lauchie added on a lighter note.

Ian glanced over at Dan Angus, but Angus's dad seemed intent on the road.

"Going to get colder," Ian murmured, letting the subject drift.

The truck returned to the muted sound of snow travel. Some areas were swept completely bare by the wild gulf wind, while others, perhaps where a patch of wild rose or stunted spruce caused a lee, were drifted three feet deep, and it was only because the snow was fresh and light that the plow could manage.

Alone, the trip would have been an impossible nightmare; in a group, it was an adventure that made the older feel younger and the younger feel older.

"It's a fine night for a game of cards," Ian said to Dan Angus. "Come to the house. These boys can visit. Be like the old days with no TV and lies to tell."

"Sounds good," Dan Angus replied. "Let's get the truck home and off the road first."

They let Lauchie out at the bottom of his driveway. Half-blinded by the blowing snow, he ran through the deep drifts toward the dim glow of his porch light.

Partway up the drive, Lauchie was ambushed by a large gray blur that bounded out of the gloom. Big paws landed on his chest, and he staggered backward, falling in the snow. He lay on his back laughing and trying to protect his face from Dog's affectionate slurps. He slowly regained his footing and ran toward the house with Dog running at his side, nipping at his sleeve.

Dog had the look of a gray-black collie, with two exceptions: he didn't have the long aristocratic nose, and he had the pale gray eyes of a wolf. He had gotten his name as a result of his untrainable nature. He lived outside by choice. He would steal anything that was edible, and no amount of reprimand could curb his cunning or cause him to feel guilt. His affectionate slurps could not be denied. He had arrived at their house the winter Lauchie was four, an almost-grown pup, lean and hungry and determined to stay.

Every day Lauchie's mom, Mary, had fed him and told him to go home. Every day he had grinned his disarming grin and stayed. She called him "that mangy dog, that useless dog, that stubborn dog, that thieving dog," and finally he became "Dog," earning and returning Mary's unconditional love. Ian said that she called him Dog to reassure herself that he really was a dog.

Lauchie's mom completed his tiny family. Uncle Ian was their neighbor. He was closer to a grandparent in age than a father, but he'd tried to pass on the values that he felt Lauchie's father would have. He was not really related; calling him Uncle Ian was a way of saying he was like family and for Lauchie to show familiar respect.

Lauchie had to kick away the snow that had drifted

up against the storm door. They had a back entrance-way, like most old farmhouses, but this entry was joined to the kitchen at one end and at the other to a small addition that Lauchie's mom used for her hair-dressing business area.

Lauchie burst into the kitchen, kicking off his boots in the general direction of the entranceway. "Mom, I'm goin' over to Uncle Ian's, huh, huh, okay?"

Lauchie's mom was washing a baking pan and watching television on the little kitchen set. The over-head light haloed her hair, which was a lighter red than Lauchie's. A faint freckling softened her features.

"Okay, but leave the porch light on and take the big flashlight. Have a fresh biscuit before you go."

"I'll have two."

"One."

"One for normal and one for the goal."

"You scored a goal! Lauchie, that's wonderful."

"No big deal." Lauchie grabbed the broom like a hockey stick. One pant leg was hitched high over his right sock, which flopped flat on the floor well beyond his toes, and melting snow ran from his hair.

"So Mom, I'm near the boards. This monster defense freak is comin' at me, Maurice, the big Indi-an. I nab the puck; duck back, flip one to Angus. He's breakin' out at center. The Moose smacks the boards, swack, smear, *umf.* I'm gone, up the ice. Angus shoots it back to me, shoots a bit long. It's okay. I make the stretch. I wind up for the big one. I don't let it go. I deke left, right, give 'er the old flip. The goalie's *messs-mer-iiizzzed*. He's eatin' my ice crystals. Goal! The crowd roars." Lauchie threw his arms up, bashing the refrigerator with the broom.

"Okay, two biscuits for saying 'I' a hundred times without taking a breath."

"And for suckering the defense monster."

"Lauchie, don't talk like that. It's not war."

"Oh, yah? They started callin' him 'the Moose' when he was ten. When he was twelve, they got him a harness so he could plow the garden. If he gets me in the corner, we're talkin' Lauchie burgers and don't hold the ketchup."

"Lauchie, I've watched Maurice from when you played Pee Wee hockey. He seems like a nice kid. Ian worked with his dad once."

"Used to be nice. Now they don't feed him before games. He chews his stick. He's like a shark. A little taste of wood and he goes into a feeding frenzy. You should've seen us."

"Wish I had. You're the one who doesn't want his mom at the games."

"Yah, well, if some guy took you—like you *had* to go—that would be okay."

His mom chased him out of the kitchen, laughing and swatting at him with the dishtowel, while he twisted around trying to get his boots back on and avoid the swats, crying out in a fake high voice, "That's my Lauchie. Why is the big boy biting his stick in half?" He escaped, pushing a big wedge of snow with the storm door. Then, unable to resist, he stuck his head back in, lowered his voice, and megaphoned with his hands, "The Moose: Two minutes . . . for . . . stick . . . devouring."

He noticed that his mom was still laughing, but there was a conflicted look in her eyes. He wondered if he should not have teased her that way. He walked back across the kitchen floor in his wet boots, feeling uncertain. "Hey, I gottah get a book on moms and how to raise them. Come on over with me. I'll break trail for you. Dog will protect you, six hundred feet across frozen northern wastes." His mom gave him another halfhearted swat, a good sign, and the phone rang.

It was Marge, calling from next door. She'd come over to Ian and Grace's with Dan Angus on the snowmobile and wanted Lauchie's mom to come over so they could all play cards.

They played three games before the power went out. Then the oil lamps were lit, the cards were set aside, and everyone fell silent in the soft glow. The stove made popping sounds and the kettle murmured, just on the edge of a boil.

"I lost my fishing helper to the woods," Ian announced. "He's makin' good money cuttin' pulp and doesn't want to leave it for the lobster season."

"I'll do it!" Lauchie hollered.

"You will not!" his mom countered.

The peaceful room tensed in a void of silence.

Marge stared at her fingernails. Dan Angus became fascinated with spoon spinning.

Lauchie's mind raced. *Mom says no . . . only thirteen . . . 'cause of my dad . . . school . . . she worries . . . do something.* He scanned the room, anxious for clues of how to plead his case. Aunt Grace gave Uncle Ian a recriminating look and went to the stove to make tea. Lauchie caught her furtive, almost shy, glance toward Mary. It was a telling glimpse. Lauchie knew that his father would not be mentioned, but the subject was on everyone's mind.

Only Uncle Ian looked relatively relaxed. "It would be good for him." He paused, looking at each adult. "Lauchie can be a doctor or a mechanic, or whatever—I'd just like him to have a little taste o' where he comes from."

Aunt Grace's hard face seemed to soften. Dan Angus looked up from his spoon spinning and spoke quietly in the hushed kitchen. "I've been having those same thoughts about Angus."

Marge shifted closer to Lauchie's mom with a questioning touch, as though looking for direction. "Mary?"

Lauchie got a quick conspiring elbow from Angus, who whispered, "All *right!*"

Mary's reply was soft, small-voiced. "You'll get him into things before he's ready—before I'm ready. He's only thirteen."

"Fourteen by lobster season," Lauchie amended, but no one took any notice of him.

Uncle Ian seemed a little surprised at the reaction, or pretended to be. "Well, I'd not spoil a fine evening over this. There's time enough to think on it. It's just that he's always helped to ready the boat, and with building the lobster traps, ever since he was a tot. Seems only natural to follow through."

"Ah, Ian, it's true you've been good to him," Mary said as she, Marge, and Grace got up from the table. Grace took one of the oil lamps, and they each carried their tea to the front room.

Now that the male and female camps were separated, Lauchie and Angus were ready to start planning for the fishing season, but both Ian and Dan Angus said that they'd have to think about it, discouraging any more discussion.

Lauchie and Angus looked each other straight and hard in the eye, like in the third period of a game, when they were down but determined to win. They slowly bumped fists.

"This's gonnah happen, Angus."

"It's like done."

They reverted to rehashing the game while Ian and Dan Angus drifted into the quiet, sparse conversation of old friends and neighbors.

Soon, amid shrieks of laughter from the women in the front room, the boys heard the phrase "feeding frenzy." Lauchie looked at Angus. Unwilling to admit to his earlier description of Moose, Lauchie shrugged in apparent bewilderment.

Ian and Dan Angus looked up at the same time,

catching each other's eye. Dan Angus gave the very slightest of nods. Ian's pale blue seaman's eyes sparkled in the soft light of the oil lamp. That look was familiar vocabulary for Lauchie, and he realized that the issue of a fishing helper had been neither casual nor chance.

2

POLITICS

Lauchie's bedroom was in the most original part of the house. Sometime in the past, the outside walls had been insulated and plastered. The interior walls were old horizontal boards, glossy and rounded from many coats of paint. The northwest wall was a half wall with a sloping ceiling. A dormer looked to the sea, a quarter mile away. A desk was built into it and beyond it, like an extended sill. The desk held a keyboard, a small monitor, and a cup of pencils, and had a small clear area for writing. Shelves on either side of the kneehole held his computer, printer, disks, books, and paper. Another narrow window looked southeast up the mountain.

Lauchie and Angus were sprawled on the bed with pencils and a shared pad. Lauchie wrote, 1. School, and said, "Our moms are gonnah be afraid we'll want to quit school for fishing."

"Nah. I want university. My dad just did high

school. He doesn't understand computers, the net—it's all strange to him."

"Angus, when he went to school, the only net was a fishing net."

"Yah, but educated old guys seem to catch on."

"We've got to convince our moms—especially my mom," Lauchie said.

Angus drummed on the pad with his pencil. "Okay. Put down the big one."

"My dad?"

"Well, he did drown off a fishing boat. Might be a consideration. Ya think?"

Lauchie rolled over on his back and stared at the ceiling, "Mom tries not to overreact to all that . . . so's I'll turn out normal. She'll be okay with it." He sat up and looked at Angus. "I've always helped out now and then with Uncle Ian. It's not like I never go on the boat."

"Sure," Angus laughed. "Sunny Saturdays. But we're talkin' every day, every kind of weather. Even my mom's a bit antsy."

"I'll look after it. It'll take some maneuvering, but I'll look after it."

"Yah, and keep talking about school. Talk about being an oceanographer or something."

"That's not new; it's what I've always wanted. What's your dad saying?"

"Nothin', same as always. You know what he's like. Probably wait till first morning, probably holler from downstairs, 'Angus, get your gear. You're goin' fishin'.'"

Lauchie rocked forward to stand up. "You've gottah

pin him down now, for sure. We're both gonnah fish the season. It'll be the best!"

Angus jumped up and they faced each other, gave the nod, and bumped fists.

"Okay. I gottah go," Angus said. "Been playing Zydag III and I can't get past level seven."

They went downstairs. Lauchie's mom was in the kitchen putting supper together. "Angus, would you like to stay for supper?"

"No, thanks. I've got a lot of homework that I have to do."

"So, what were you two plotting?"

Lauchie looked bewildered. "We weren't—"

Angus looked innocent. "—plotting anything."

"Ever since you two could walk, you never bothered going up there unless you were planning some crazy scheme."

Angus got busy with his coat and boots and scooted out the door. "'Night, all."

"Lauchie, would you set the table for us?"

"Sure."

As Lauchie set, his mom put out food. It was a cold-weather kind of supper, with boiled potatoes, corned beef, cabbage, and turnips.

"Were you talking about fishing, you two?"

"Yah."

"I don't want you going."

"*Mommm.* My best friend's going to be fishing this summer. What am I supposed to do?"

"I don't want you to go, because you're too young.

You're thirteen years old. And Marge feels the same way about Angus."

"I'll be fourteen. 'Sides, if Angus's dad says it's okay, then Angus will fish."

"Well, in this house it's just you and me, and *I* say. And I say no!"

"So what would my dad say if he were here?"

Mary slammed the table with her fist, her face suddenly set, her voice strident. "That's unfair—really unfair! If your dad were here, we'd talk about it together, and we wouldn't necessarily come to the same decision as Dan Angus—or handle it the same way. He's not here, and I'm doing the best I can—which is not too shabby, by the way." Mary's face began to soften. "Lauchie, it's not just one simple thing. It's about school and fishing and. . . . I've never kept you from the sea, but I don't particularly want to look out my kitchen window and see the storms come up when you're out there."

"Ah, Mom, hardly ever anything happens."

"'Hardly ever' isn't good enough for me. 'Hardly ever' has already happened to this family."

They were sitting with their plates steaming, not eating. "It's not fair, Mom. Angus will be telling me what a great day it was on the water, maybe seeing some whales, maybe getting a monster lobster. I'll tell him I went strawberry picking, got chased by a giant mosquito or somethin'."

The beginning of a clamped-off smile tugged at the corner of Mary's mouth. Lauchie spotted it with relief. "Well, I don't know why you'd suddenly start picking berries," she said. "You've never picked them for me before."

"I'd pick 'em 'cause my life's over and it doesn't matter. If Angus works and I don't, I'll be shamed. I can't believe you'd do this to me. I want to make some money. I can help out . . . and get some stuff for myself, too."

"Sure, and get to like it. Lauchie, fishing gets to people, gets in your blood. It's admired, and traditional, but it might soon be all over. Draggers are getting bigger and bigger, belonging to big companies. Quotas are getting smaller. About all that's left for the small fisherman and a two-man boat is lobster, and even that is in danger."

"Mom, I can't believe you'd think that I'd leave school. I know some older kids who quit—it's like they're livin' in the past or somethin'. . . . How come I can help in the woods? How come I can help build traps? How come I can even go out and help fish, but I can't make a job of it?"

"'Cause you're thirteen years old, that's why. You're not supposed to be working."

"Yah, well, when we need firewood in the fall, it's no problem. Besides, Uncle Ian says that nobody can build as good a trap as I can, and he's the best fisherman. We'd catch more lobster than Dan Angus."

"Your dad caught more than any of them."

"Yah, see? See?"

"Lauchie, you'll not gain points on my honesty."

"Mom, I want to do this. It's very important."

"The answer's no. Now eat. Your supper's getting cold."

"I'm not eating. I'm on a hunger strike."

Mary smiled. "Now, that truly worries me. I'll tell Aunt Grace, just in case you forget yourself."

Lauchie ate slowly, pushing the food around on his plate. It seemed tasteless and his stomach felt weak, as if he were in a state of fear or horrid humiliation. Now that the possibility of fishing with Ian had come up, he could no longer conceive of not doing it. He knew that everything he did and especially everything he said would have to be carefully tailored to further his cause.

"Lauchie, I don't particularly like eating in silence. It's rude."

"I don't feel like chitchatting. You treat this like I'm asking to go to a movie or something. This is important to me. I don't want to talk. I don't want to eat. I feel lousy."

Lauchie pushed back his chair and almost stumbled from the table. He felt even worse seeing the hurt look on his mother's face, but there was no way to retreat from his position. He went out to the mudroom, threw on his Ski-Doo suit and boots, and went outside.

Dog greeted him at the porch. For as long as Lauchie knew, Dog had been his friend, playmate, and confidant. His usual greeting was to leap at

Lauchie. But sensing the mood, Dog only nudged him with his shoulder, receiving an almost absent-minded ruffling of his ears in return. They walked through deep snow between the big apple tree and the old barn that was just used for storage now, past the snow-buried garden, then southeast toward the foot of the mountain, where the field ended and the woods began. Lauchie headed toward the beginning of their woods trail, which they shared with Ian to service both their wood lots. It was near their fence line, marked on Ian's side by a snow-covered rock pile and on Mary and Lauchie's by a big white pine with an old weathered stump near its base. This was Lauchie's thinking place. Both his house and Ian's were blocked from view by their barns, and the only light visible was the flash of the lighthouse on Margaree Island, three miles off shore. The late-winter sun had set and the last red tints had vanished, but it was not yet fully dark. Fields blanketed in purple snow sloped to the road and on toward the sea. The sky over the pack ice was a deep, saturated blue, and the gulf ice glowed dimly beneath it. A brightening behind the mountain indicated where the moon would soon rise.

Sitting on the stump, Lauchie felt much calmer. He wasn't thinking so much as waiting for the horrible disappointment to dissipate. He stroked Dog's ears, comforted by both the softness of his fur and his quiet patience. He reached into his pocket and pulled out his lucky stone. It was red, sea-polished, and looked like a bear. He'd found it two summers before and always kept it in his pocket, but tonight it held no solace and he put it away. A light breeze keened in the pine above him and skiffed powder along the surface of the snow. The dark blue sky deepened toward black.

The full moon first peeked, then slowly rose above the mountain, lighting the distant ice, then rushing closer as the angle rose. Lauchie was warm in his suit. One hand was bare but buried deep in Dog's fur. He had come out not so much to make a plan as to escape an unbearable feeling. Nothing had changed, yet he felt better, sensing that his dilemma would, somehow, be resolved. The moon rose higher, grew smaller, soft yellow turning to cold, hard chrome. Tall weeds cast sharp, elongated shadows on the bright snow. The shadows of the barns were absolute, dark and harsh, their roofs aglow. Bare silver branches of the apple tree veined the sky above Lauchie's barn.

The cold solitude seemed to both simplify and emphasize the importance of the issue. Lauchie stroked Dog's head and scratched his ears. "I want to fish. I want to know everything I can about it." Dog watched Lauchie, as though he understood his words rather than just his feeling. "Someday I want to study the sea and maybe help make the fishing better. But for now I want to fish." Lauchie stood up, drew a big breath, put his glove back on, and made a swatting gesture at Dog's nose. Delighted at the easing of Lauchie's gloom, Dog sprang up in an explosion of snow, playfully nipping at Lauchie's glove. Lauchie gave in to Dog's exuberance. "You're a good friend, Dog. The best."

They zigzagged in an ambling course back to the house, roughhousing and kicking up light powder snow that drifted ahead of them, glittering in the moonlight.

When Lauchie went in, Mary was watching television.

"Good night, Mom."

"Good night, hon."

Lauchie awoke, turned off his alarm, and lay staring at the ceiling, savoring a few moments of inactivity in the warmth of his bed. He enjoyed a short few seconds of normal waking before remembering yesterday's problems. He sighed and rolled slowly out of bed, got dressed, and went down for breakfast.

"Here's your toast; butter it while it's warm."

Lauchie took the toast and slouched into the kitchen chair. He muttered a sullen thanks, then slid the plate of toast toward the butter.

"Do you want meat sandwiches or peanut butter for lunch?"

"I don't care."

"Lauchie, if I'm good enough to make your lunch, you could at least tell me what you want."

He stared at the tabletop. "I don't care. I probably won't eat it anyway."

Mary stared at him, tight-lipped, a blush of anger

rising to her cheeks. "I've about had it with this attitude."

"Mom, my best friend's going fishing this summer. I'm not. This summer will be the biggest embarrassment of my life. Guess what? It doesn't make me happy."

"Lauchie, sometimes I have to make decisions for you. That doesn't make me responsible for how well you handle them."

"Yah, well, it's not like I want to feel bad. I just do. I'm letting an opportunity slip by."

"We'll talk about this more. Now go to school."

Lauchie was halfway down the driveway, before he realized that he'd forgotten his lunch. He shrugged and continued. Dog walked beside him. They would separate at the end of the driveway and Lauchie would walk about a thousand yards to Angus's driveway, which was the school bus stop.

The road was clear, but plow-packed drifts still lined the sides, and windblown powder sifted off their tops, shimmering in the morning sun, laying long white, shifting diagonals across the road. The ice-covered sea seemed to dance and shift as the early sun shone through low-blown snow.

Angus was already there, waiting with a couple of younger kids from the next farm down the road. He gave Lauchie a jab in the shoulder. "Hey, mopo, what's with you?"

"Mom's still totally against me fishing. It's a major battle."

"We've gottah change that," Angus said. He pumped the air with his fist. "I talked to my dad. I'm fishin'."

"Great. We're halfway there."

"No, I'm all the way there. You're still at the starting gate."

"Yah. It's going to be hard."

Angus shrugged. "Just keep pushin'. That's what I'd do."

"Not with my mom; she's as stubborn as I am. She'll just dig in her heels and get mad. She's already pretty ticked off at me."

"Well, you better do something."

"It's gottah be something new, something that tips the scales."

Their bus came. They got on and headed for the back seat.

"We've got a game Wednesday," Angus said as he flopped down.

"Yah, Moose again. How come the smallest guy in the league has to play against the biggest guy?"

"Easy, Lauchie; he's left defense, you're right wing."

"Sometimes he plays like he doesn't even notice I'm there. I really want to beat him."

"Hey, we're talkin' a whole team here."

"No," Lauchie said. "I want to beat him, personal, like last time. He's boarded me too many times."

Angus shifted in his seat. "We're supposed to have our science project ideas ready this week," he said. "We've gottah think of something we can do together."

"Yah, I was thinking that we could make a tide, like the Bay of Fundy. We could trace the shape off a map, get depths, and make it in a big pan or somethin', with concrete."

"It won't make a tide."

"No, dingbat." Lauchie said. "You just make a small wave and watch it get higher when it goes up the narrow bay."

The bus was traveling along the shore road, passing the wharf where Lauchie hoped to fish. The pack ice had fused, freezing the gulf solid. Great blocks of ice had been upended against the wharf in some earlier tide or storm, creating a sparkling jagged wall twenty feet high. The early-morning sun lit the base in turquoise green and rimmed the upper edge in glaring gold. Lauchie glanced at the spectacular scene, barely seeing it.

"Why not collect statistics on how many times a one-hundred-and-five-pound kid can be checked by a one-hundred-and-sixty-pound kid and survive," Angus suggested. "Could call it runts and giants."

"Or canners and markets."

"What's it got to do with lobster sizes?" Angus asked.

Lauchie gazed out over the endless dazzling ice. He sat a little bit straighter and turned to Angus, grinning. "Nothin'—just an absativily, posilutely great idea."

Angus looked confused. "You are crazy!"

Lauchie pounded Angus's shoulder. "Our science

project. They always separate the more valuable large market lobsters from the smaller canners. So the fisheries department must know how many pounds of each are caught every year. But what they don't know is how many lobsters made up those weights. If helpers on boats made those counts, it could be really valuable information, a database for other stuff."

"But school will be over by then."

"So what? The preparation can be the project. How could my mom keep me out of the boat if I designed the project?"

Angus looked at Lauchie, gave him the nod with exaggerated respect. "All right! How can they give us a bad mark when it's for the fishing industry?"

"Our project could be the pilot project. Maybe next year all the boats will do it. We could be famous."

Angus leaned back, stretching his legs down the aisle. "Sure, famous for causin' extra work for the fishermen. They'll run us off the wharf."

"There could even be a count of how many under-size lobsters get thrown back. That would be helpful, too."

Angus drew his legs back, tapping a beat with his toes. "Could be a definite winner for your mom," he said. "It's a good project, too."

The bus was grinding to a stop by the school. The younger kids ran to the front, jostling each other to get out. Lauchie and Angus took their time walking down the length of the bus. Angus tapped Lauchie's shoulder. "Let's go sell it, genius," he said.

The idea was a big hit at school, generating a lot of

discussion about fishing. It was perfect for Lauchie, guaranteed to be discussed in the small community. The design and preparation would be given a mark as a project, and Lauchie and Angus had to promise to present their findings when they returned from summer vacation. Lauchie checked it out with Ian, who was skeptical about the fishermen ever doing it, but he suggested refinements that would avoid time loss while fishing. Lauchie decided to let his mother discover his plan rather than force it upon her and risk a fast and negative response. With this in mind, he told Angus to tell *his* mom all about it, emphasizing their joint involvement and trusting that it would get to his own mom very quickly. It did.

The next day, when Lauchie came home, it was instantly obvious that his program was loaded and rolling.

"So, Lauchie, why am I hearing from Marge about your very interesting science project? Why aren't I hearing it from you?"

"Well, if you really want the truth, I planned it that way."

"Because?"

"'Cause I wanted you to think about it a bit before you gave one of your irreversible no's."

"Are you suggesting that I'm stubborn?"

"Let's just say that you have very strong convictions."

"And this project that you cooked up isn't just a scheme to get what you want?"

"I've always said that I want to study the ocean.

This is exactly the project that I should do. Right?"

"The way you handled this, I think you should study politics. But okay."

Lauchie froze, his ears suddenly ringing, his heart pounding, afraid to query that 'okay.' "Okay what?"

"Okay you can fish. *And* do your project—which had better be real, by the way."

"It's real. It's real. Wow! Why the sudden change? Never mind . . . I don't want to ask."

"It wasn't sudden. Seems the whole community wants you to fish. I can't do a simple haircut without discussing your alleged summer job. Your special science scheme was just the last straw."

Lauchie's pulse still pounded. His face was flushed, and he could barely follow what his mom was saying. His instinct was to flee before something changed. He began edging out of the kitchen, toward the living room, feeling goofy and awkward. "Thanks, Mom! Gottah call Angus."

"Can I take that to mean, Thanks, you're the most understanding and wonderful mom of all time, and I promise to take great care of my humble, worthless self while fishing?"

"Yah, sure. You're the best. Gottah go," Lauchie said, and he fled to the living room to call Angus.

3

RITUAL

Ian and Lauchie had been busy for the last two months repairing old traps and building new ones, Ian through the day and Lauchie helping after school. Much of the work had been completed during the winter, but there was always a bit of a rush before the season's start. If traps were lost or damaged in a storm, back-up traps would be needed. Lauchie had always helped at this stage. When he was a little kid, Ian used to take him to his trap shed, down by the wharf. Often Dan Angus and Angus would join them, and the men would work together on their traps while Angus and Lauchie played together with scraps of lath and string and rope. Lauchie had fond memories of the trap shed, warmed by a wood stove on blustery March days.

Now it was late June and school was out. Everything was ready for opening day, and opening day was tomorrow. Ian had dropped by, hollering as always when he walked in, "Hello, Mary dear."

"Don't you 'Mary dear' me," she answered with a false glare. "Come to take my boy, have you?"

"Ah, well, he'll be no boy when I'm finished with him."

Even though the issue was long over and settled, Mary suddenly grabbed Lauchie, hugging him with one arm and beating him softly on the back with the other, a dishtowel clutched in her fist. Lauchie felt confused and embarrassed.

Ian shuffled about. "Ah, now, Mary."

"Get away, you old fool. Get out, the both of you. Go down to the wharf and tell him lies about the old days."

Lauchie was even more confused seeing his mom both wet-eyed and smiling. He and Ian fled out the back door, Ian laughing and Lauchie feeling half guilty and half relieved. He looked at Ian for an explanation. "What was that about?"

"I'm only sixty-three," Ian said, "I don't pretend to understand. Perhaps she's very proud of something beginning and just as sad about something ending." They walked along the path to Ian's. Ian paused and looked out to the sea. "We'll just go down to the wharf for a bit; sniff the breezes."

They climbed into Ian's old pickup and headed for the wharf. There was no real need to go, Lauchie knew, yet it felt like exactly the right thing to do.

The sun was bright, but the day was cool, with a westerly making enough chop to send spray over the wharf. The air was filled with harbor smells of kelp and bait and diesel oil. The traps that usually lined the wharf before setting had been stacked ashore in fear that the wind might get stronger. Seven Cape Islanders were pulled up on the wet slip and propped securely with bars and old fishing crates. Each was as unique as the person who owned it, yet similar in design with distinctive near-vertical bow stems, deep keels, and the simple tough craftsmanship of an open working boat. The largest was only twenty-eight feet in length, with a twelve-foot beam, and the smallest, a proportional twenty-one feet. At rest on the steep slip, the boats had the look of colorful beached whales. Each one had an old rubber glove pulled over its exhaust stack to keep water out of the engine, and the upturned fingers wiggled and twitched in the wind, seeming to wave at the clear, hard sky.

Ian parked at the foot of the wharf and they got out. Lauchie leaned on the truck's fender looking west, out of the harbor, into the wind. He could hear Ian's footsteps in the gravel behind him retreating toward his trap shed. He almost wandered out onto the wharf but restrained himself, thinking that that was a kid kind of thing to do.

For Lauchie it seemed as though the harbor were holding its breath. It felt as though the sights and sounds and actions of tomorrow had already happened and only the intervening time held them at bay.

Ian hollered, "Bring the two broken traps from the truck."

Lauchie turned and saw Ian watching at the trap-shed door. "He knows," Lauchie thought. "He feels it, too."

The shed was small, about sixteen by twenty-four, with an old red asphalt-shingle roof and grayed wood-shingle sides. The door faced the sea, and the only window faced south, toward the mountain, to catch the winter sun. Beneath the window a workbench made of two rough planks ran almost the length of the shed. An old wood-and-coal stove stood in the center and beside it, an ancient, tiny table saw. A black-smith's vise was bolted to the end of the bench. It was dark after the bright outside light, and the air smelled strongly of fresh wood laths and rope. Ian reached for something on a shadowed shelf above the window, sliding it into his coverall pocket. "It's dank in here. Let's take these traps out front to sit on."

They propped the traps against the outside wall and sat with their backs against the sun-warmed shingles. Ian was silent for a while, and Lauchie qui-etly looked out to sea. "Tomorrow you start work. I'll pick you up at a quarter to five. You'll be ready. You'll make eighty dollars every day we go out. I'd guess you'd give most of that to your mom, and about time, too." Ian was trying to sound gruff and formal. Lauchie tried to look serious and adult.

They were enjoying a ritual that they had never spoken about, though it had been tacitly anticipated by both—Lauchie's graduation to working fisherman.

"Yes, sir," Lauchie said, trying not to grin.

They sat in silence for a few more minutes, listening to the wind sough against the side of the shed. Ian broke the silence. "You can start with the oilers that you used to wear helpin' out. I saved you this," he said, handing Lauchie a bait knife in a well-oiled sheath.

It was slim-bladed from many sharpenings and had an "L" burned into the hickory handle.

"Your dad's," Ian almost grumbled. "When your mother had to sell the boat, I kept the knife for you. It's just a tool. It'll finish wearing out soon enough. I just didn't want a stranger usin' it."

Lauchie searched for the right words, then simply said what he felt. "Thanks, Uncle Ian. I'm glad you did that."

They sat a few minutes longer. "Come to the house for a tea and biscuit. Grace has something for you. The old gossip's been at the phone all week tellin' that you'll be fishin'."

Ian closed the trap-shed door, dropping a wharf spike through the hasp to secure it. As they walked to the truck, Lauchie slid the knife in his back pocket. The ground seemed distant, as though he were taller.

Aunt Grace's kitchen was warm and spicy with the smell of fresh-baked apple-cranberry pie. She was clearing the table when they came in, and Lauchie guessed that his mother had been there. It crossed his mind that they, too, had their rituals, and the idea fascinated him.

Aunt Grace went to the sideboard drawer and took out a pair of fisherman's gloves that she had knit for him. They were of rough gray wool and oversized. They would get thicker and tougher as the seawater shrank them, working like a diver's wetsuit, allowing the water through, then holding it in to warm it up. They were the only kind of gloves that would work in cold seawater. "Lauchie, dear," she said, "I made you these gloves to protect you from the cold, harsh sea." Lauchie held the gloves in his right hand while he hugged Aunt Grace.

"After all these years she makes the best gloves," Ian boasted. "Falls asleep knittin' but never drops a stitch."

Lauchie thanked Aunt Grace, ignoring Ian's teasing, moved by the work and care that she had taken and knowing that it was her way of giving him the nod.

The gloves and bait knife were tools. No matter how simple they were, to Lauchie they represented the difference between real work and just helping out. A kid helps out the best he can with what's at hand; a workingman has his own gear. The bait knife had been his father's, a tool he'd handled and used daily, and Lauchie took it as a sign that his dad would have approved. He, too, would use the knife every day, cutting up mackerel for bait.

When Lauchie left, he lingered alone in Ian's entranceway, slowly pulling on his rubber boots. The floor was covered with worn linoleum that had always been there. The room had its own familiar smells, the rubber scent of oilers and boots, an earthy musk of potatoes and turnips, a hint of gun oil from the old double-barrel hanging by the door. There was something deeply reassuring and comforting about that familiarity on this special day.

Lauchie walked across the patch of lawn and past the barn to the path through the marsh grass. He could see the slight arc of the gulf from west to north, the horizon softened by distant waves. Plumes of white spray flashed at the tip of Margaree Island, three miles out. The long narrow fields tilted northwest toward the sea in sloping ribbons of rich young grass, the green broken only by brushy stone piles and lavender patches of wild rose bushes. A line of shrubby bushes followed the creek in a meandering diagonal. To the southeast, the mountain rose, brightened by the young new bud growth of spruce and new leaves of hardwoods. The white shingles of his house glowed brightly at the foot of the mountain, a field's length below the last trees.

Dog met him at the halfway point. He was in his greeting pose, tail up and chest down, with his big paws thrust forward. He regarded Lauchie with his wolfish gray eyes and his tongue hung sideways to the left, resting dangerously over his big eyetooth, giving him a reckless, laughing look. His next move, Lauchie knew, would be to launch himself in mock attack. Lauchie headed him off by quickly stooping and grabbing him around the neck. "Tomorrow I start fishing—a big day for me. You probably know all about it." Dog listened, as he always did, then gave a quick twisting wiggle and slurped Lauchie. "Let's go see what's to eat for a kid and a dog."

Lauchie was relieved when his mom didn't ask about the day. It would have been impossible for him to explain. It had been a day of little rituals. After supper they cleaned up and made his lunch. He got in the way more than he helped, but doing chores together had always been their way of sharing when they felt untalkative. When they finished, Lauchie sat at the table. He felt tired but feared he'd never be able to sleep, and his excitement was more like pain than joy, like the night before a birthday for a little kid. His mom sat down across from him, a second cup of tea in her hand.

"Honey, when Ian brought up the idea of you fishing with him, he said that he just wanted you to have a taste of where you came from, and that's exactly what frightened me the most. It sounds corny to say that fishing gets in your blood, but it's like that."

"I know, Mom. It's special, and I want to do it. I want to do other things, too, but I need to do this."

"I want you to do it, too. I just want you to realize that now fishing is a world of million-dollar draggers and factory ships. You have a lot of choices, but fishing a twenty-four-foot Cape Islander might not be one of them."

"Yah, well, draggers can't fish lobster."

"No, but when Ian started fishing, they fished everything from a small boat. He had no other choice. Everyone farmed a bit and logged a bit and fished a bit. There was lots of lumber and lots of fish. Now there isn't much of either."

"I hear you, Mom. Cowboys don't ride horses anymore."

"Strictly mopeds." Mary smiled, then went to her work area and retrieved a large plastic bag. She threw it to Lauchie. "I got you new oilers, so you won't have to look like a clown in Ian's old hand-me-downs."

Lauchie jumped up, ripping at the bag. "Yellow! Incredible! You're the best, Mom."

"You like yellow?"

"Yah! Orange looks like road-crew guys or somethin'. I couldn't wear orange." He squirmed into the yellow rubber overalls, jumping from one foot to the other. He pulled the rubber jacket on and zipped it up, strutting around the kitchen.

"They're a bit big, but you'll want a heavy sweater under them. They were the smallest I could get."

"Thanks, Mom."

"Well, you and Ian might think that you're getting away with something. Don't go out thinking I'm not proud of you. You'll be the youngest at the wharf. Now, give me a hug and go to bed."

Lauchie crawled into bed, thinking of the day past and the day to come. Soon his breathing matched the tempo of the surging waves on the distant shore. He fell into a dreamless sleep with none of the trouble that he'd feared.

4

FIRST DAY

He awoke scrambling for the alarm clock in the dark. His memory of falling asleep was vivid, as though the night had been only a moment's inattention. He dressed quickly in jeans, heavy socks, and a heavy wool sweater, and crept down the stairs, amazed at how the old house creaked at four-thirty in the morning. He wondered if it had creaked the same way for his father.

In the kitchen a cheddar-cheese-and-biscuit breakfast was wrapped beside his lunch with a note:

> *I know you won't stop to eat, but*
> *you'll be hungry after the first load.*
> *Tomorrow, brush your teeth. GOTCHA!*
> *Love, Mom*

Lauchie laughed to himself, realizing that he had been caught out. He stuffed the food under his sweater and squirmed into his rubber boots. Then he grabbed his gear and slipped out into the chill, dark morning.

He heard the familiar squeak of Ian's storm door, six hundred feet away, clear in the early-morning air, and then the hollow clunk of the truck door. Lights stabbed into the black sky, arcing up and down as the truck rolled over driveway bumps. Dog loped beside him like a dark shadow. At the road Dog gave Lauchie's hand a quick nudge with his nose, and Lauchie ruffled his ears. With a low, throaty woof, Dog strode back up the drive. He had dog things to do.

"You could have at least brushed your hair," Ian growled as Lauchie climbed in. Lauchie glimpsed a grin in the dim cab and decided to say nothing.

At the wharf, two pickups were parked at the head of the slip with their lights shining down where the boats would be launched. Figures flashed into the light beams, then disappeared back into the darkness as the men readied the seven boats that were on the slip, each boat resting on its side, wedged against old fishing crates. A faint glow of false dawn etched the mountaintop in the east, but down on the slip it was dark, and the slap and *glonk* of waves sounded loud and mysterious. The air was dank, filled with west-wind secrets of fish and kelp.

The fishermen all worked together to slip the boats. Each one was righted on its keel; then with pushing, prying, cursing, and even laughter, it would suddenly give way to the sea-greased planks. Everyone ran with it down the ramp, struggling to keep the boat upright while trying not to slide on the greasy timbers, until it hit the protection of the sea with a great splash that glowed briefly white.

By the time all the boats were tied up along the wharf, it was light enough to see. Everyone began loading traps and gear on the pickups to run down to the boats, and to stack on the wharf for later loads. Though their boats were tied side by side, Angus and Lauchie barely noticed each other. Intent on performing well, they raced to leave the harbor.

Ian chuckled over Lauchie's impatience to get loaded and away. Finally, they were ready: boat loaded, engine idling. Lauchie needed only to untie the bowline and climb down.

Ian hollered, "We forgot the lobster gauge! It's on the dash."

Lauchie quickly looped a bight on the big iron cleat and ran toward the truck, anxious to get this last chore done. He'd taken about three steps when it hit him. They were only setting the traps today; they didn't need the gauge. He'd almost turned to inquire when the full impact fell like a rock in his gut. He'd been had. He felt an instant surge of embarrassed anger. His new status had been snatched away. He was the dumb kid. He turned, flush-faced, forcing a grin.

Ian watched, both concerned and amused, but even worse, Dan Angus was watching from his boat, enjoying the gag, while Angus looked askance, comically adjusting his hat. Lauchie hung onto his grin, freed the bowline, and climbed down the ladder, pushing the boat free as he jumped aboard.

"It was done to us all, boy, one way or another," Ian said in a quiet, firm voice.

The little twenty-four-foot Cape Islander crept out of the harbor, low bowed with a heavy load of traps. They passed between the big rock, darkly submerged on their left, and the L of the wharf's seaward end. Lauchie stood ready, with his feet spread wide for balance. They rounded the tip of the wharf.

They were out.

The boat sprang to life. Her trap-laden bow reared high as she swung around, quartering the first chop and settling into the next with a determined smack, sending a sheet of icy water into the air that folded back with the wind, driving at their yellow oilers, streaming foamy from the tightly lashed traps.

Lauchie tasted the sea salt on his lips and looked back at Ian. They both grinned, lurching in unison as Ian pulled her about in a trough and settled in for the outside Marsh Point Grounds.

Lauchie scanned the charcoal sea, his legs adjusting to the cant and roll of the boat. He could feel the tension along the deep-biting oak keel, the only straight line in the boat, its backbone, its center, the point of resistance between wind and wave and will. He didn't think these things but sensed them as a reassuring resonance and memory in his feet and legs. As the shore fell behind, their tiny boat became the center of a circle of sea making its way free of the land.

Lauchie held up three fingers, then six. Ian nodded; that meant three traps, six fathoms apart, Ian's standard set. Lauchie took out one trap, opened it, and added some crazy ballast—stones that would add weight until the traps become waterlogged. He opened the hundred-pound bait box and removed a mackerel, which he cut into thirds. He pushed a piece onto the barbed bait stick in the trap's bottom. Next he took the short snout line from the trap and tied it to a long coil of half-inch rope. He measured off six fathoms to space the next trap, measuring the rope against his widespread arms. He coiled the rope on top of the trap, placing the trap on the stern deck, and then added two more traps in the same way and attached a numbered buoy. The set was ready to go. Ian grabbed the first knot and inspected it, nodding with satisfaction.

They were still moving out. Lauchie looked back to shore. The surf's white line along the foot of the cliffs was bright against their darkness. He could see his house and Ian's tucked in at the foot of the mountain, and morning fog that had collected in the mountain's creases rolled down the stream beds in silver coils, spilling out in long gray columns over the sea.

The sun was just rising over the mountain, and it made the fog flash suddenly white as the first rays caught it. The sea, which only moments before had been sullen and dark, was transformed into a dashing sheen of glassy green and sparkling white foam.

The engine sound changed to a ragged idle, and the boat began to wallow in a slow troughy turn, pitching abnormally with its load of traps.

Lauchie watched for Ian's nod, got it, and pushed off the first trap. It hit the water with a splash, and the coil ran out, pulling off the next trap, and then the next. Lauchie stood back from the ropes. He held the buoy high and threw it well clear of the boat. If a loose coil grabbed a hand or foot, he'd do a deep dive— probably too deep, too fast, and too cold to survive.

Lauchie prepared another set while Ian brought them around for the next run. He looked back at the first buoy in their wake. Not long ago, these waves had been stilled beneath pack ice. No buoy had been on this water since last year, and here was the first, bright and red and sparkling, like a promise of a good season to come.

They worked back and forth for twenty sets of three traps each until the boat was empty. They still had eighty sets to pick up and put out. Freed of the load, the boat looked and acted as she should. Ian poured them tea for the ride back to the wharf, and Lauchie dug out his cheese biscuit to eat on the way. He leaned on the bow-coaming, with his head in the wind, drinking the best cup of tea he'd ever tasted.

At the wharf, a lot more people had arrived, friends and family who'd come down to help load the traps and bait sets. The atmosphere was festive but just a little frantic.

Lauchie grabbed the bowline and climbed up the ladder. It was warm now, especially at the wharf. He had discarded his heavy sweater, but he kept his new oilers on, feeling that they marked him as a real fisherman among those who were helping out for just the day. The traps that they could not take on the first load were stacked along the seaward side of the wharf, ready to go, each fisherman using the area where he docked. It was Lauchie's job to lower each trap to the boat, using its own snout line as a rope. Ian stacked and packed them to his satisfaction.

Up on the wharf, the normally clear area was a chaos of loads on pickups and stacks of traps, rope, and buoys. Where Lauchie needed to load, Billy Barr was starting a stack with traps off his dad's truck.

Lauchie and Billy had been enemies from the first time they had met, for no reason that Lauchie knew except that he was small enough for Billy to beat up. Billy had bulk and liked to use it.

"Hey, Billy, we need to load here," Lauchie said.

"Yah, well, my old man says put 'em here, so I'm puttin' 'em here."

Lauchie decided to start loading anyway. He walked behind Barr's truck to get at Ian's pile, felt a push from behind, stumbled, and turned to see Billy looking meaner than his normal mean. He advanced on Lauchie, poking him in the chest. "Think you're so big, eh? Fishin' the season, eh? Fancy new oilers, eh?"

Billy was backing Lauchie into the trap pile, and Lauchie knew that he had to get out of there or take some abuse. Billy was a clutching, smothering kind of fighter, and fear of that violation of space and movement enraged Lauchie. He didn't want to look like a dumb scrapping kid on the wharf, but the only way out into the open was through Billy.

Lauchie stopped backing up. He stomped the heel of his rubber boot down hard, raking Billy's shin and crunching his instep, and followed through with a driving right to his belly. Billy gasped. It wasn't much of a punch. The stiff oilers hampered Lauchie. But with the combination of surprise and fury, it was enough. He sensed Billy giving way. Billy backpedaled, managing only a couple of wild swings. Unaccustomed to defense, Billy now had his weight working against him. His wild swipes were more attempts at balance than punches. Lauchie slipped a punch and parried with a satisfying jab to Billy's nose.

"Hold it!" Ian bellowed from the ladder. "You're here to fish, not fight."

The world around Lauchie snapped into focus, and he realized that he was on the open wharf, surrounded by spectators of whom he'd been unaware. He flashed a silly guilty grin, looking contrite. His apology sounded foolish. "Sorry, Uncle Ian. I had trouble getting to the traps."

He heard someone comment, "Tough little booger, that" as Billy sidled away from the crowd and climbed into his dad's truck, wiping his bloody nose on his sleeve.

Lauchie finished the load, walking the traps

around Barr's truck. He glanced once more toward the pickup and climbed down the ladder to the boat. As they neared the end of the wharf, Ian started chuckling.

"What are you laughing at?"

"It's nothing," Ian said.

"Come on, what is it?"

"Well, I shouldn't say this, but when I came up off the ladder—it was like I was seein' your dad an' his a few years back."

"They didn't get along?"

"Like oil and water. Old Billy and young Billy are much alike, I suspect." Ian grinned but quickly looked astern to conceal his mirth. "Doesn't mean I condone fighting," he mumbled, turning forward again. "Didn't know you were that good."

"I wasn't that good. I was that scared."

"Well, you whupped him. He took off like a hurt dog, rip-eared an' tail-tucked, slinkin' t' the woods to lick his wounds." Then Ian laughed; his big laugh that he reserved, Lauchie knew, for those special times when life was delightfully just right. Lauchie laughed, too, laughed with relief, feeling the incident drift to the less specific past, taking the fear and tension with it.

They were clearing the harbor and the sounds of engine and sea made further conversation impractical. "Yah," Lauchie told the wind. He didn't know why he did that; it just felt right.

By noon, they were on their fourth and second-to-last trip. The wind that had been steadily rising now slacked off a bit. "Breeze's down," Lauchie noted.

"Yes, and I don't like it at all."

"Why not?"

"This time of day," Ian explained, "it should be steady. It'll rise again harder, a few points to the north, and I'm not likin' the sky to the west. We could get a bit of a blow. We'd best eat now, on our way back in."

They left with their fifth and last load, running west past Shag Rock. Now the wind seemed to be strengthening and shifting. They had three sets remaining when Ian, watching a squall to the west, decided that they'd better make a run for it.

"Make up the sets as we go!" he yelled. "Forget about the bait. We'll drop them on the run and move them later." Lauchie saw Dan Angus's faster boat coming up behind them, from the River's Mouth Grounds to the west. His traps were going off his stern like depth charges. Lauchie scanned the sea about them. All the boats where heading in, tending to pair up in a buddy system. Everyone, he knew, would be watching for the telltale raincoat lofted upon an oar that signaled trouble.

Lauchie worked fast. When the traps were ready, Ian scarcely slowed the boat until the first trap hit. Lauchie jumped clear, well forward of the unraveling loops, holding the buoy above his head. The traps were torn from the stern deck, ropes hissing and zinging, the buoy snatched from his hand to disappear in sinking troughs, seeming so distant when it reappeared on the frothy crests. Dan Angus's boat overtook them just as they'd both cleared their traps.

Lauchie mimed hurried, anxious rowing motions, earning a nod from Dan Angus and a grin from Angus as they throttled back to stay abreast. Then he began to stow everything that was loose under the bow deck. Angus was doing the same on the other boat.

When he was finished, Lauchie was surprised at the changes that had occurred in only a few minutes. The squall to the west was racing up the coast toward them, darkening the sky. The west sea was a malevolent cold steel color, and the distant silvery breakers seemed obscure and unreal in the blowing rain and spray. Looking east, he could see the distant wharf and the flashing white breakers hitting the breakwater, still bright in the sun.

Wild gusts tore at the sea, raking spray and spume from the crests, layering the air with flying briny foam. The boats were edging out from shore now, side by side, two troughs apart, quartering the waves; sliding almost sideways down the troughs, then climbing through sheets of spray that the wind threw across the open decks. Soon they were out beyond the grounds in deeper, better water. They passed well outside of Jonathan's Grounds, and the shallowest lobster grounds looked like a breaking beach emerging from the sea.

Lauchie glanced back. Ian grinned, looking rakish

and wild, water streaming down his weathered face. Lauchie laughed, surprising himself. He thought he should be terrified, but he a felt a part of the storm. They were surrounded by the power and strength of water and wind. It felt good.

He began to study how Ian picked his way through the chaos, always knowing which wave was ready to die and which was ready to rear up. Lauchie saw a big wave form and grow, obscuring the bow of Dan Angus's boat, tumbling and breaking above their decks, dwarfing men and boat in scale. They disappeared as their boat troughed, and then reappeared on a rising swell, ethereal in the flying spray. Dan Angus nodded and powered ahead. They were in position now to make their run for the wharf.

They watched Dan Angus hold to the wave, neither breaching forward nor falling back. The wave lengthened and rose, swallowing others as it built. Its crest rose higher, and its trough dropped lower. It began to break up early, just as they were passing the L of the wharf. Lauchie could see Angus looking small and distant at the bow and Dan Angus, hard at the wheel, keeping her tight to the wharf, clawing for depth, avoiding the treacherous rock just south of the entry that now sent brilliant geysers skyward.

The wave began to crumble, and they cornered with their stern awash, disappearing behind the wharf.

Ian found a good wave and held the boat on the backside to make their run. In the deeper water it was not so bad, but as the bottom shelved up, the wave grew. It grew until Lauchie feared the trough would bare the bottom. The little boat clung to the shoulder of the great wave, her bow pointed glistening at the sun and sky, her stern chased by the dark maw of the trailing trough and the low black clutch of the chasing squall. The wave's arms stretched like massive wings to left and right, great glassy green hills of water, lacy with spume, whelming and rising.

As they passed the L, Lauchie heard the huge left arm smash, thundering against the breakwater, saw tons of white water hurtle gleaming into the air, shadowing the sun behind them. The wharf, normally high above, was now level with the little boat, and the wharf's surface was awash and gleaming with the streaming remnants of the broken wave.

They were in.

The great wave died with a frothy, hissing sigh, gently lowering the boat. Crashing waves on the breakwater and shore sounded distant and hollow to Lauchie, as though he were hearing things in a vacuum. His heart was pounding, and he held the bowline in a tense grip.

Dan Angus's boat was already on the slip, and as Lauchie jumped for the greasy timbers, Angus was coming down, dragging the big donkey winch cable. They hooked on to the bow-stem ring and guided it up the slick ramp, then helped to wedge it with fish crates and poles. The work done, they greeted each other with proud grins.

"A boat ride," Angus said.

They walked up the steep slip. Lauchie felt a pleasant weariness from the work and the excitement of the day. When they reached the gravel lane at the top of the slip, the first big wind-driven drops began splattering on their backs. After the feel of the sea, the ground felt hard and lifeless. They both looked down the coast at the wild water and the sheets of approaching rain. It looked interesting, remote, like an old picture on a wall.

"Boat ride," Lauchie agreed.

5

SEA GIFT

Ian and Lauchie worked with the comfortable trust of those who had worked together for a long time, the result of years of Lauchie helping and watching, an apprenticeship that began when he was old enough to pass a nail or fetch a board. Now they had the added cadence of daily routine. The harshest part of the season was over, and so was their first setback: a broken trap hauler that meant three days of hand hauling three hundred traps while they waited for the replacement part. Lauchie's memory of aching muscles and throbbing hands became a feeling of pride and confidence. The water had warmed, and they no longer needed gloves. Now Lauchie's hands were work-hardened and calloused.

Ian had held off on the tradition of moving the traps to shallower water as it warmed. There had been another big storm. Their traps remained undamaged, while those who had moved in suffered losses and tangled sets. Now Ian was prepared to move their deepest traps to shallower water, moving a few each day.

They still had about thirty traps to haul, down by Shag Rock, to the west, and their bait net was en route, so they decided to tie up to the net buoy for tea before pulling the net. Huge rounded swells still rolled, remnants of the storm just past. They were the kind of waves that caused action on shore, but on the sea they gave a smooth easy ride.

The bait net was set far out, almost off the tip of Margaree Island. Ian said it was over a deep gravel bottom where they used to catch big halibut on hand-held lines. The gravel was caused by some quirk of tide and current as they ripped between the island and the mainland. It was a good place for a bait net and, Lauchie suspected, a likely place for a wayward salmon to pass.

Lauchie was drinking his tea and looking down into the water as the boat swung on its anchorage. He saw a buoy pass slowly far below, visible only because the boat's shadow shielded the sun's glare where he was looking. He got the gang hook from under the bow deck. It was just three wharf spikes bent into hooks and welded together with an eyehook and a few fathoms of rope. He lowered it to the depth that he thought was needed and waited for the boat to swing back. "There's a buoy down there," he explained, noticing Ian's curious look.

Soon the buoy reappeared, but he missed it. The

gang hook lagged behind the boat as it swung, giving little chance to line it up, but on the return swing he had time to maneuver, and he easily snagged the other line. He let the hook run up the line until it caught on the buoy.

Lauchie always felt a sense of mystery pulling traps; this was a mysterious trap. He loved to watch a trap as it first appeared, dim and purple gray, suspended in the depths by the long curve of rope; then slowly changing to dark blue green as it rose, then light turquoise green, rapidly turning to its true color as it burst from the sea to be hauled, streaming water onto the gunnels. He also enjoyed the mystery of opening a trap that only moments before had rested on the bottom, eighteen fathoms below.

This trap had traveled perhaps a mile along the bottom, caught in some strange current of storm and tide, until it had been released in deeper, calmer water far from the grounds, submerging the buoy on a line that was shorter than the depth.

As it came into view, Lauchie and Ian could see it spinning, as though the snout line were fouled. As it rose higher, they saw the broken bottom slats that had released the ballast. The front end was stove in and had worked the bottom like a scoop; a tail of sand and debris drifted from the trap as it rose. Something larger was caught in it, perhaps a rock. When Lauchie hauled it, dripping, over the gunnels, Ian remarked, "Looks like Dan Angus's line and buoy. At least we saved that for him."

Lauchie reached in to grab hold of the rock. It felt strange. It was black and scaly-looking and roughly cylindrical. He shook it; it contained something. They both studied it, noticing marks in the black scale like traces of canvas weave.

"It's an old crock that's been sealed up with something—tarred canvas, I'd guess," Ian said. Then he said something strange. "Whatever it is, it came to you, Lauchie—a sea gift."

They decided not to tamper with the strange container until they got home, which made good sense, but made it hard for Lauchie to finish the day.

They pulled the net. Hand hauling a net is hard heavy work, but on a day like this they could let the boat and the sea help them. As the boat fell into a trough, they gathered in as much line as they could, and then wedged it against the gunnels. As the boat rose on a crest, it would pull more net to be gathered in as the boat rode down the next trough.

Lauchie watched the net slowly appear, every strand forming a graceful curve into the sea, bracketed by the countering curves of the mesh. Far below he could see dim flashes of silver, which became brighter and clearer as they rose, slowly taking on the forms of fish. Some were gaspereaux headed for the river and eventually the lake where they would spawn. Most were spring herring.

They hauled the net, clearing the fish into a bait box as they went, then let the boat drift, carefully letting the net back out. As the last of the net slipped beneath the surface, Lauchie tossed the coiled buoy rope and then the buoy. This one was different from the trap buoys: it had a vertical shaft, with a weight on the bottom and a small red flag on top. The elevated flag made it easy to find from a distance and warned others that there was a net below. Ian started the motor and headed for Shag Rock.

The cormorants were on the rock with their wings stretched out to dry and their long necks stretched straight up, looking like solemn black totem pole figures. Behind them the charcoal-colored cliffs reared to the sky, lending a spooky darkness to the shoreline.

A flock of gulls followed every boat for the cast-off bait and, if you weren't careful, what they could steal from the bait box. Lauchie was baiting the first set when a big, scruffy old gull landed on the bow. He'd been blinded in one eye, and he regarded the bait box with his head turned sideways like a parrot. Lauchie could see his sharp amber eye darting from bait box to Ian.

"Zachariah, you old pirate! I thought you were dead," Ian yelled. He got a small herring and threw it to the gull, which snatched it from the air, then uncharacteristically stayed on the bow to eat it. "His disability check," Ian grumbled. "I swatted the old thief with a rope a couple of years ago. Thought I'd done him in."

"Does everyone feed him bait?"

"No, and you'll not be tellin' about me doin' it. It's

between me and the old thief," Ian answered as Zachariah flew off with an ungrateful screech.

Lauchie laughed, and Ian glared at him with a look not unlike Zachariah's, making Lauchie laugh all the more.

"If you say a word about it, you'll not fish another day on this boat," Ian threatened.

When they got in, most of the other boats were already there. They tied up next to Dan Angus's boat. Lauchie helped winch up the catch and made sure that everything was stowed before he brought up his mysterious find. Angus was on his dad's boat, hosing down the deck.

Lauchie called to him. "Angus, come see what I caught."

Angus looked up at the wharf. "Seen enough big lobsters for today. Got one so big he near chased me out of the boat."

"Come on. This is something special."

Angus coiled the hose and stowed it, looked over the neat deck, then scampered up the ladder. "Whaddah you got?"

Ian was standing by Lauchie. Other fishermen realized that something was happening and drifted over.

"Shake it," Dan Angus said. "If it gurgles, it's for me."

"Already did," Lauchie answered. "It's not Jamaica rum."

"A pity, that. Then we've no interest in it," Dan Angus declared.

Rodie Jim was about Ian's age. He'd just tied up and joined the group. "Perhaps you found treasure," he suggested with a grin. "There's stories enough about three-masters with tattered sails and boogans and ghoulies comin' ashore in long gray coats, with cutlass and musket, in the full o' the moon."

"You believe that?" someone asked.

"Well, on a stormy night, with the snow swirlin' at the windows and the house timbers creakin' and the stove poppin' and a good man tellin' it, with a toddy to share, it makes perfect sense," Rodie Jim said with a grin and a gasp for air. "Otherwise, no, I believe what I see."

"Well, your grandfather saw 'em," Ian said, looking at Rodie Jim. He took a great breath, glanced about at the grins of anticipation and dropped his voice into storytelling mode.

"On Donk's Mountain he were, coming late from a hunt with a young buck slung over his back, when an unearthly fog, hoary and foul, rolled in from the sea—and no breeze to push it. He heard them approaching, mewling and whining like winds in the riggin'. In a swirl of the gloom he saw them all waitin'. A-rent and a-tatter were their clothes, drab and moldy. Faces like suet they had, and the stench o' dead beasts hung all about 'em. Sentinels they be, numbered seven, chill phantom spirits o' poor murdered sailors, kilt to guard treasure, beneath their vile bones.

"'There be booty for ye,' one wretched wraith keened, 'if ye'll take, in the name o' the devil!'

"'I'll not do that!' he roared, makin' the sign—and there, before his horror-struck eyes, they all tarnt to dust, and the taint o' them was bestrewn in a whorl o' dank fog."

Ian scanned his audience with a satisfied grin. He leaned a little forward for emphasis, his hand at his side, half-curled in relaxation as though pulling a rope. His weathered face and pale seaman's eyes seemed to exaggerate his comically wicked expression. Lauchie had heard the story many times before, yet he smiled, deeply contented to be there on the wharf watching Ian's antics.

They went back to discussing Lauchie's find. "Why not bust 'er open right here?" someone suggested.

"Ah, no," Ian explained, looking very serious. "Could be a boogan in it, just waitin' to get out." He picked his sweater off the winch arm, where he had hung it. He slung it over his shoulder and walked down the wharf. "Well, I might as well feed these two," he said, as though he were not curious himself.

"Come on, Angus; let's go," Lauchie said.

It had taken forever to get off the wharf, but now they were sitting in Grace and Ian's kitchen. Lauchie slid the strange cylinder onto the table in front of him.

One end had a definite lid, and Lauchie began scraping off the black crud until a seam could be seen. He pried it with the knife tip, and a piece of pottery chipped out. Then, with a pop of imploding air, the seal broke, and the lid came free, releasing a stale odor like decaying paper.

Lauchie reached inside and felt something wrapped in stiff cloth. He pulled it out. It looked like old canvas, brown and rotted, and the remnants of some ancient twine lay over it. It crumbled at his touch.

Lauchie's hands trembled as he unwrapped it, breaking the canvas at some of the creases. He knew then that he was holding an old gun still wrapped in another layer of oil-treated paper. He stripped off the ancient paper to reveal a beautifully embossed flint-lock pistol. The handle and fore stock were polished and oiled walnut. The metal working parts were steel, but the guard and breach were brass inlaid with silver.

One side said:

London Gunne Co.
Smith's Lane
London, England

The other side said:

Capt. James Ross
The Lucy Irene
Glasgow Towne
1612

The inscriptions were surrounded with oak fili-gree. A silver cap was fitted to the butt of the handle and to the end of the tamping rod, which was brass and fitted under the barrel. Lauchie traced the inscription with his finger. "Who was he? Why'd he do this?" He turned it in his hand, feeling its weight.

Angus stood close to Lauchie, staring at the gun. "Lauchie, can I see it?"

Lauchie gave Angus the gun, carefully, two-handed. He felt numb, the voices around him vague, distracting. He heard Aunt Grace on the phone, calling his mom.

Lauchie reached back into the container and pulled out a handful of lead shot and a small cracked and dried-out leather pouch. He carefully set the shot on the table and handed the pouch to Ian. "The powder."

Lauchie reached in again to get a last lead ball and noticed that the inner walls of the crock were not walls at all but coils of stiff old paper. He carefully coiled them tighter and lifted them out. He stood holding them in upturned hands, uncertain what to do. Ian quickly removed everything from the table. Aunt Grace wiped the table and dried it.

"Wait," she cautioned. "I'll put a clean tablecloth down."

When the table was covered, Lauchie set the papers down. He carefully separated the first sheet. It was blank on both sides, and he placed it so that the arc curved upward and it rested on its ends. The second sheet was the same, but he could see old writing on the third, and he placed it the opposite way, so that it could be read.

Lauchie heard his mom arrive, but he didn't take his eyes off what he was doing. The first two sheets of paper were much darker than the third, having taken the brunt of the deterioration to protect the inner sheets from the destructive air. The writing was ornate, and the ink had a wispy, faded look. The thick old paper was brown from aging and freckled with even darker oxidation marks, but most of the words were legible.

"This is a very old and delicate thing," Mary said. She gave Lauchie a quick sideways hug. "I think you've found something very special."

Lauchie glanced quickly at his mom, then back at the old paper. His voice sounded distant, distracted. "From the bottom of the sea."

6

THE OLD LETTER

Lauchie began reading. *"August, This Year of Our Lord, 1632."* He looked up. "Nearly four hundred years ago! *Little Sea Dog Island, One day's sail W.S.W. off The New Found Lands, eight days out of Jamestown."*

"Could put him hereabouts," Ian mused.

"In fear that I'll not see civilization again, I write this down to . . . seal with . . . Can you make that out?"

"Pitch," Mary traced along the faint script, *"to seal with pitch . . . in a ship's crock and wrap the whole in . . . tarred sailcloth."*

Lauchie continued, *"I shall bury it 'neath a cairn on the point of this wee isle with the ship's pennant, that any passing soul might know our fate."*

"Under what?" Angus asked.

"A cairn is a pile of rocks," Ian explained. "Like a marker."

"For London we were bound," Lauchie continued, *"on the* Lucy Irene, *homeport Glasgow, out of*

Jamestown and the Barbados with cargo of rum, molasses, and tobacco, on a northward course to catch the high trades off The New Found Lands.

"Beyond the island forming the southern arm of the great gulf of the French colonies, we were taken by pirates."

Everyone seemed to shout at once.

"Extreme!" said Angus. "Southern arm of the great gulf, that's us—good ol' Cape Breton."

"You're right. He's talkin' about here."

With Angus peering over his shoulder, Lauchie continued, *"Our crew was put on the attackers' foul ship and I was retained on the* Lucy Irene *to treat the pirates' wounded."*

"He was right there with the pirates!" Angus yelled.

"Angus, let me read. *Small cannon, shot, powder, arms, and a small chest were all that were brought over in slings, from the pirates' ship.*

"The pirate leader was now in command of a much larger ship, and undermanned. Of his crew, some were wounded, and others had sampled the cargo's rum. Though storm threatened in the northeast, he sent men aloft. We were soon under way on a broad reach, the shore falling off sou'west to larb'rd."

Lauchie glanced questioningly at Ian. "Larboard," Ian said. "The old term for the left side of a boat, what we call port side."

"She was well healed over, her bowsprit seeming to dive for the crests like a great marlin about to sound; the shadow of her mighty masts keeping pace beside us.

"The wind backed again, from the north-nor'east and stronger. We were running before the wind.

"I was sent below to care for the wounded, but noted the effects of a building storm as I worked. It was fully dark when I again came on deck. Storm lamps cast a feeble light. Wind gusted, rain lashed. The sheets were heavy and wet, the rigging treacherous and slick. Two masts had been cleared, but the main stood under sail, taking the storm's full rage and might. All men were aloft. Now in the storm's full grip, the deck was awash, the sea thundered, rigging keened. Wet sails flashed like mirrors in the forked lightning.

"Rocked by a gust, I grabbed the lashings on the main mast. My hand fell upon splintered wood on the forward side and I pulled myself around to investigate. A load of grapeshot had rent a great shattered chunk from the mast. I looked to the starb'rd side, cleared the streaming water from my eyes, and stared in horror. Three of the six shroud lines had been severed from the abuse of the shot and the pressure of the storm. As I stared, the fourth line went with a loud crack, and the others, under greater stress, let go almost at once, whipping the heavy lines into the darkness. I dove for the starb'rd rail and tied myself to it.

"Through the passing sheets of rain I watched the main mast cleave from the damage at its base to the mains'l nest. The yardarm swung fore and aft, the crack opening and closing like a pale, gaping wound. Seamen fell to their deaths in sea and on deck, their cries lost in the deafening storm, their bodies swept

from the flooded decks. The aft brace let go, and with it the others followed.

"The great mast fell to larb'rd like the mighty tree it once was, at first slowly, then faster and faster. Deep into the sea it plunged. Canvas and rigging like a giant sea anchor attached to the broken ship by tangled ropes and the larb'rd shroud. She spun like a cork, the fallen mast canting her deck to the point of rolling, while the storm's fury drove it back in the direction of its will. Ropes snapped and cleats tore free, ripping the dragging mast clear. The crippled ship righted with a sickening lurch. She was a soulless hulk, helpless before the wind.

"Above the wail and moan of rigging, I heard the crashing tumult of shore or reef.

"I knew that I and any still aboard were surely lost. I watched in horror as the foredeck planking peeled skyward before me. Stressed tenons and cracking ribs shrieked like the ship's last scream, and then all was obliterated as I was buried 'neath a roiling wall of water."

Lauchie paused to sip his tea. His hand trembled; he was breathing quickly, as though he'd been in that storm, as though he'd wakened from a nightmare. He passed the remaining pages to his mom. She didn't begin reading immediately; everyone sat for a moment in shocked thought. Lauchie got up and looked out the kitchen window above the sink. He could see the bright, calm sea at the foot of the fields, but in his mind he saw a storm-wracked ship. He returned to the table, the echoes of the ancient storm ringing in his ears.

Mary began to read. *"I awoke thinking that my back was on fire and I couldn't move. I realized that I was still tied to a strip of the ship's rail, my face pressed into a pillow of rotting kelp, the hot sun burning my back. I felt a tug and an easing of the ropes and rolled over to look into the grave eyes of a big native. He stooped over, casting a monster shadow, and lifted the heavy oak railing free. In his left hand was a big rose-colored quartz knife. I knew I was about to die.*

"Sheathing his knife, he pointed to himself saying, 'Anoogwet Wokwis.' Then, making a sort of all-around sign, he said, 'Micmaci.' He retrieved a basket of blackberries from the ground and taking a handful, squeezed them so that the juice ran down my dried throat.

"'Thomas,' I croaked, pointing to myself.

"Anoogwet Wokwis wears a simple breach cloth of soft-looking leather and moccasins of the same material."

Mary looked up from the letter. "He's talking in the present tense now."

"You're right, Mom. Maybe it means that they're still together, like while he's writing, he's looking at what Wokwis is wearing."

Lauchie took over the reading again. *"He has a storage bag on his hip, and his knife sheath hangs on a thong from his neck. His moccasins and bag are finely decorated. The leather is a pale, creamy color, darkened in places by wear. My battered and fouled clothing seems awkward and rough in comparison.*

"Though every movement reveals new scrapes and bruises, I have no serious injuries. All about us cargo and wreckage are strewn, and a major part of the hull has washed up down-shore. There are no signs of survivors. The ship was probably driven some distance after she lost her mast."

Lauchie tipped the page toward his mom. "Look, the ink's kinda different. I think he wrote a bit, then stopped, then wrote some more. . . . This is amazing."

"He could be talking about down by our shore," Angus added.

Lauchie continued reading. *"We've spent three days stripping the wreck and storing what we could on shore. The captain's quarters were intact, but a shambles, and there I retrieved my doctor's bag, and the paper and materials for this letter. We found a beautiful pistol that, I feel, has no place in this land; but being too fine to destroy, I shall place it with the letter. The small chest that had been brought aboard holds a collection of gold coins, silver pieces of eight, and European jewelry."*

"Pieces of what?" Angus asked.

"Pieces of eight are old Spanish coins," Ian explained. "They were divided in eighths, and people sometimes made change by slicing off a part of the coin. That's why they used to call a quarter 'two bits.'"

Lauchie continued. *"In a chamois bag, I found a huge emerald of strange cut, and I believe that this great stone was New World treasure. I shall bury the coins in some safe place, but the jewelry I intend to give to Anoogwet Wokwis's people, the great emerald a gift for a chief. These items have little value here. I'll enjoy giving them as gifts. One fine ruby ring I have already given to Anoogwet Wokwis. It was too small for his finger, so he strung it on his knife thong.*

"The best discovery, from the captain's quarters, is a fine glass. At first, Anoogwet Wokwis was frightened by it, but he soon realized its potential. I indicated that it should be his, and he is well pleased. With the glass we studied cormorants to the west drying their wings on a shaggy-looking rock that jutted into the sea."

"'Shaggy-looking rock!'" Angus shouted. "Like *Shag Rock*, just west of the wharf."

"Whole coast is mostly rocks," Ian cautioned.

"He'd call it what we call it," Lauchie said, continuing to read. *"By drawing in the sand, Anoogwet Wokwis showed me that the big island is called Sea Dog Island—Boktusum—and the small one is Little Sea Dog Island. In a similar manner he illustrated his name. Anoogwet Wokwis means Gray Fox.*

"I shall hide the treasure at the highest point of Little Sea Dog Island where . . . What's this?"

Mary and Angus tried to decipher the words. *"Beneath a small cairn . . . a sink a hole,"* Angus tried.

"I sank a hole," Mary suggested, *"just south of a large square rock."*

Lauchie looked over, continuing to read. *"This letter, with a map, I shall seal in a ship's crock and place it by the shore with the ship's pennant, that any passing soul might know our fate.*

"Now I close the longest letter that I've ever writ. Tomorrow I shall become a doctor once again, to a new people.

"God willing,

"Thomas Mac Dougall,

"Ship's Doctor."

Lauchie looked up. The familiarity of Ian and Grace's kitchen only emphasized the uniqueness of the moment. Lauchie struggled with the strange feeling. "I can't believe it's real. It's not a story. He did his best to tell what happened. . . . Now it's four hundred years later."

Mary rested her hand on Lauchie's arm. Ian nodded in silent agreement. Even Angus seemed subdued.

Lauchie looked at Angus. "I wonder how he did, with the Micmacs," he said. "He liked Anoogwet Wokwis."

"He might have met up with Europeans eventually," Ian said. "The first settlement was Scots, in 1629, but it was way over on the other side, and the French booted them out. But fishermen were probably coming here long before that."

Mary laughed. "Ian, how do you know this stuff?"

"Well, I've lived hereabouts a long time."

Lauchie turned the page and stacked it on the others, then saw what was beneath it. "It's a map! It's the map, a real treasure map."

It had been drawn with a very fine pen. It looked like a harbor, but it didn't look much like their harbor. It was protected to the west by a long point and to the north by a small island and the bulk of the coast. The island almost touched the shore at the back of the harbor and to the north. The water between shore and island was probably a sea pond. That was definitely not there now.

"The big island and the coast sure look like Margaree Island," Lauchie said.

"Sea Dog Island. Isn't a sea dog a pirate?" Mary asked.

"Yah," Lauchie agreed. "But the doc just thought Anoogwet drew a dog. But I bet he drew a wolf. The old name for Margaree Island is Sea Wolf Island."

"That clinches it!" Angus yelled, loud in his excitement. "So where's the other island?"

Ian spoke up. "There used to be a long point at the west end of the harbor. It was longer than it is now even in my time. Those big boulders on Jonathan's Grounds are probably part of the old point. The old folk said they remembered cows grazing halfway to the island, though it was probably more like a tenth of that, I'd expect. Time changes the land. It could even be Port Hood Island that they came to. There's a sea pond at Port Hood."

"Doesn't look like that, though," Lauchie protested, tapping the map. "Port Hood's thirty miles away."

"Nah, the place is here. Somewhere right out that window," Angus said. "That's why you found it here."

"I wish the letter wasn't poorest on the first and last pages," Lauchie muttered. "There's something missing there."

"Well, it does look like it could be 'cairn,' like a rock pile," Ian said.

Mary stared at Lauchie and Angus. "Now, listen up, you two. Lauchie found a valuable antique and what is probably a very valuable document, but I don't want to see you going crazy over some impossible treasure."

Ian looked up. "Perhaps you should mind your mother, Lauchie. I don't know where you'd start. You need a small island, close in, and a big island, and a sea pond and a long point. That's just not here."

Lauchie looked away, out the kitchen window, staring hard at the sea, as though the intensity of his gaze would provide an answer. "It's there."

"Hey, don't fret. But that treasure is going to be our fishing license some day," Angus declared, which got him a concerned look from Mary.

"Lauchie," Mary said, looking directly at him. "I think that we should contact the museum to find out how the letter can be properly looked after. I think that you should let a historian look at it. It would be terrible if it got damaged."

"Okay, but it has to stay a secret."

Grace finally spoke up. "I can see there'll be some nonsense for a while."

Lauchie looked up at Aunt Grace, worried about her tendency to gossip. He imagined her already edging to the phone. "Aunt Grace," Lauchie said, "this is a real, absolute secret!"

"Oh, Lauchie, I wouldn't tell anyone," Aunt Grace reassured him.

"I know," he said, "but this time that includes 'Don't tell a soul but,' and 'Don't breathe a word but.'"

Everyone started laughing. Aunt Grace tried to look outraged but gave it up, laughing herself. Lauchie gave her a hug, knowing that they had a pact.

7

LITTLE MOOSE

Lauchie and Angus were at Lauchie's studying their copy of the old letter. Unwilling to subject it to a copy machine, they had each copied sections of it by hand and stored the original in tissue paper. Lauchie had then taken their handwritten version and typed it on his computer so that they could print it out. Now they were struggling with the directions that would lead them to the treasure. "'Beneath a small cairn, I sank a hole, just south of a large square rock,'" Lauchie read. "There's something wrong here. He'd build the cairn afterward, so why say he dug beneath it?"

"He just means that's where it is, under the cairn."

"Nah. It's somethin' else, or we're not reading it right. This last page was tough to read."

"We're stuck," Angus said.

"I wonder if there's a Micmac tale about the doc,"

Lauchie said. "He said he was going to live with them. He would have been kinda special, wouldn't he?"

"Forget it, Lauchie. We don't really know any of those guys."

"So what? They just go to a different school. I see the guys we play against in town sometimes."

"How about your favorite defenseman, the Moose?" Angus suggested. "He might know." Then, "Nah. He wouldn't know. Probably wouldn't say even if he did."

"What's to lose? Let's call him."

"Lauchie," Angus said. "We can't tell anybody about this."

"We don't have to. We won't talk about treasure. We'll just ask some questions."

"Okay, then, you call him," Angus said. "His school's in the Micmac community. Look him up."

"I know where he lives, out by Skye Mountain. Ian pointed his place out one time. Ian knows his dad." Lauchie went to his computer and found Moose's number online. Then he took a deep breath, looked at Angus, and dialed. His conversation was brief and respectful. He left his number and hung up.

"So?"

"That was his mom. She said he's out oystering, but she'll get him to call when he gets back. She said it'd probably be a couple of hours."

"Didn't know he fished oysters."

"Well, he does," Lauchie said. "I think they raise them on shallow grounds. It's like fish farming."

"Lauchie, we've gottah be real careful here. We can't tell him about the treasure."

About four-thirty the phone rang, and Lauchie ran to the living room and grabbed it. "Yah, hi. Is that Moo . . . Maurice?"

"Yah. You called."

"Uh, Maurice," Lauchie stuttered, "I've, uh, got Angus with me here. We're from over on the other side. We play hockey against you guys."

"Yah, yah, I know you—small, fast, and tricky."

"Thanks, just trying to survive. Anyway, we're, uh, wondering if you know someone who knows the old Micmac tales."

"It's 'Mi'kmaq.' Like 'meeg-em-ach.' Sure, lots of old stories. Why?"

"Well, we came across a letter, about a ship's doctor who went to live with the Mi'kmaqs."

"Mi'kmaq is plural. There's no 's.'"

"Sorry. Mi'kmaq. Anyway, the letter's from 1632, and we thought there might be an old story about it."

"That's old! It'd be kind of interesting."

Lauchie's voice faltered. "Yah, well . . . I'm not sure we can show you the letter, uh . . . yet."

"Let me get this straight," Moose said. "You want me to get some information for you, but you don't want to tell me why?"

"I can tell you later, I just can't tell you now," Lauchie said.

"Look, I don't really know you guys, except on the

ice. People wanting to know about the Mi'kmaq usually want something. I'm wonderin' what you want all of a sudden. When you're ready to talk about it, let me know."

"The letter talks about some *stuff*," Lauchie said. "We want to find it."

"Mi'kmaq stuff?" Moose's voice rose a notch. "Because there is no way that I'm gonnah help locate old Mi'kmaq stuff, outside of the nation."

"It's not Mi'kmaq stuff, but the letter talks about a Scot and a Mi'kmaq who became friends."

"And?"

Angus made an impatient grab for the phone, but Lauchie pulled it out of his reach and slapped his hand over the receiver. "Chill!" He returned to the phone. "Maurice?"

"Yah."

"We need your help with this."

"I'm sort of interested, but you're going to have to give me the whole story, or nothing happens."

"Okay," Lauchie answered. "Let me talk to Angus. See what we can do."

"Yah. Call me."

Lauchie hung up. He did a palms-up grimace and shrugged.

"I knew he'd be like that," Angus said.

"Ah, come on," Lauchie answered. "We're asking him for help but not tellin' him the whole story."

"What, are you on his side?"

"No, just seein' it from his side, is all."

"Sometimes I don't understand you," Angus said.

"We've been friends since we could walk and talk, and you don't understand me?"

"Yah, well, you go wimpoid sometimes."

"Understanding the other guy isn't 'wimpoid.'" Lauchie paused a moment. "I think we should trust him with the letter, maybe just hold back on the directions."

"What if he wants in or tries to beat us to it?"

"No way," Lauchie said, "this is just us. Besides, he lives about thirty miles away. He doesn't know the area around here."

"We'll only show him a copy," Angus said. "We can just leave out the parts that could tell where the treasure is."

"Yah, but those are the parts that we want help with, dingbat. We've gottah take a chance. We should show him most of it. Talk to him, then decide."

"Okay," Angus said. "But if he gets hostile—if anything seems strange—we stop."

"Okay."

"You call. You talked to him before. You're like buddies."

"Thanks. Get on the extension line, downstairs, but keep quiet."

When Lauchie called, Moose answered right away. "I don't take back anything that I said. I don't know you well, but it sounds kind of interesting."

"Well, same here." Lauchie tried to sound reassuring. "We thought maybe you could help. I can't tell you everything yet."

"Yah, well, I'm not sure I can offer you anything," Moose said.

"So?"

"If you want to come over tomorrow afternoon," Moose said, "we can talk, maybe I can help, maybe not. I've gottah work the oysters in the morning."

"Sounds good. I have to work the morning, too."

"Doin' what?"

"Fishin'," Lauchie answered. "Angus and I are fishin' lobster. Different boats, though."

"Hey," Moose said, "wannah trade some lobster for oysters?"

"Nah, but I'll bring you some. How many?"

Moose chuckled. "A dozen nice canners would be good, and a couple more for a wise old lady."

"What?"

"We'll talk," Moose said. "We'll see. You know our place?"

"Think so. Place with all the heavy equipment out back."

"Yah, that's it. My dad does earth moving, digging basements and stuff. Like I said, I've gottah work the oysters in the morning. What time you want to come?"

"We're done fishing by noon . . . then lunch. It's about thirty miles . . . maybe we can get a ride partway. Let's say two or two-thirty."

"Okay."

"Thanks, Maurice."

"Well, you got me curious. Bye."

Lauchie thought that Angus would still be mad. But he came back from the other phone grinning. "Lauchie, you pulled it off. We gottah get seven canners each."

"And you think I'm weird?"

"What are you talkin' about?" Angus made a palms-up not-guilty gesture. "Hey, we're going to Moose's place. Have big pow-wow."

"Ever wonder why he might have an attitude?" Lauchie said.

"Okay, okay, I hear ya."

The next day Ian drove them partway, with their bikes on the back of the truck, because he had some errands that took him in that direction. They unloaded their bikes at the chainsaw repair shop.

"Thanks, Uncle Ian."

"Call me a bit before you're ready to leave and I'll come and pick you up or meet you halfway. I don't want you riding home in the dark."

When they arrived, Moose was working outside. He was wearing monster brown coveralls and using a shovel to chip dried mud off the treads of his father's bulldozer. He paused and offered his hand, in a serious, formal way.

"Long ride. You must be hot."

"Not bad," Angus said.

"We got a ride partway with my neighbor," Lauchie explained.

"I've just gottah service this big ol' baby. My dad's

hauling gravel today, so the dozer's home. They take a lot of maintenance." Moose walked up the driveway. Lauchie and Angus walked beside him wheeling their bikes. Moose's house was much like Lauchie's, an old story and a half with white shingles. The driveway continued past the house to a Quonset equipment shed, where a barn had probably once stood. They rested their bikes against the side of the house, and Lauchie handed Moose the lobsters, which were in a damp burlap bag. "Best get these out of the heat, maybe dampen them down."

Moose took them, grinning and making weighing motions. He pulled some loops from a hose that was hanging on the side of the house, ran the water until it was cool, and sprayed the bag. He handed the hose to Lauchie, and, pointing up the mountain, behind the house, said, "Good water, gravity-fed from a spring." Then, "I'll be right back." He went into the house with the lobsters.

"Sure goes on about the dozer," Angus said.

"Hey, relax," Lauchie said. "He's just a bit nervous, same as us."

"Bet he starts it up, just to show off."

When Moose returned, Lauchie was shaking wet droplets from his hair, and Angus was leaning forward, drinking from an arc of water that spouted from the hose.

"I've gottah finish up here. It'll just take a few minutes," Moose explained.

"Can we help?" Lauchie asked.

"Nah. Machine like this looks tough, and it is, but there are places you have to be careful with when you're cleaning it."

"Hate to just watch," Lauchie said, feeling uncomfortable.

"By the time I found another shovel I'd be done. You could get me that can of hydraulic fluid from the truck, though—and a rag."

Lauchie and Angus went to the truck that was parked to one side of the driveway. They got the five-gallon can of hydraulic fluid, a big funnel, and some oily rags. Behind them they heard the snort and snarl of the big dozer starting up. Moose was rolling it back. He cut the engine and the sudden silence rushed in like a vacuum. Angus grinned wickedly, while Moose showed Lauchie the location of the hydraulic cap. They topped up the fluid while Moose cleaned the section of track that he had rotated to the top.

"Wipe up any that overflows. That stuff's bad on the paint," Moose said. He stored the shovel behind the seat, gave the dozer one more inspecting glance, dinged the fuel tank with his knuckle, and grinned. "Fuel's fine. Okay, we're outtah here." He pulled off his coveralls and stuffed them behind the seat of the dozer and walked back to the hose, washed his hands and face, bent over and hosed his hair, then sprayed his work boots. He combed his fingers through his wet black hair, which was long and straight. "That's better. Thanks for the help."

They were suddenly all staring at each other with nothing to say.

"Nice dozer," Angus offered.

It was such an obvious weak attempt at conversation that they all laughed. The respite was brief, but gave Lauchie a starting point. "So . . . we found an old letter that was sealed in a ship's crock and lost for nearly four hundred years. Our families and my next-door neighbors are the only people who know about it."

"Because it talks about some stuff, you said. Is this stuff *Mi'kmaq* stuff?"

"No," Lauchie stared at Angus. Angus rolled his eyes and shrugged. "It's, ah . . . like . . . treasure."

"Where do I come in?"

"The guy who buried the treasure," Angus said, "was sort of saved by a Mi'kmaq guy. He said he was going to live with the tribe."

"So . . . " Lauchie shrugged, looking at Moose, and said, "Maybe you guys know something about it."

"If you don't know anything, why would we Mi'kmaq know anything?"

"I don't know," Angus said. "We just thought that maybe there was an old tale or something. We're kind of stumped."

"Don't see how I can help. But I sure am curious. Let's go out back. There's a picnic table under an apple tree there."

As they settled around the table, Lauchie pulled a copy of the letter from his back pocket. They heard a screen door bang, and all looked up to see a little girl, about four, coming down the wooden steps. She frowned in concentration as she carried a big bottle of Coke and a stack of four glasses. Moose jumped up to help her. "This is Clarissa, my little sister."

"Mom says you shouldn't be rude!" Clarissa told Moose.

"Yah, thanks. Now scram. We're talking here."

"This is my table, too. I don't have to, and I want some Coke."

Moose grinned, filling the glass that she held out. Clarissa sat in the grass under the end of the table. She began humming, to show that she wasn't listening.

Lauchie kept the last page and handed the rest to Moose. "Maurice, you gottah promise not to talk about this."

"Yah, sure." He set the sheets facedown beside him. "You might as well call me Moose. Everyone else does." Clarissa's head suddenly appeared at tabletop level, with her wrists against her forehead and her fingers splayed out like miniature antlers.

"Little Moose," she stated solemnly.

"Get outtah here."

She disappeared under the table again.

For a moment, neither Angus nor Lauchie spoke. Clarissa began humming again under the table.

Moose leaned forward, resting his elbows on the table. He looked from Angus to Lauchie. "So?"

"Well, it like mentions treasure. We want your help.

. . . I promised Angus that it would be just him and me lookin' for it."

"You think I'm gonnah steal your treasure?"

"Ah, come on, Moose," Angus said. "We're just trying to be straight here."

Moose looked up into the apple tree for a moment, then briefly glanced at Angus. His stare moved to Lauchie, and held for a beat.

"Listen. I grew up hearin' the old Mi'kmaq stories and wisdom, and sometimes they make a lot of sense. They teach people how to act, what to watch out for— stuff like that. We've gottah think Mi'kmaq for a moment here. You imagine that this is all a piece of good luck, and I guess it is, but the luck is to be given a kind of test or quest. It's yours, not mine. Why would I want to take another man's test?"

"For treasure," Angus quipped.

"Sure," Moose laughed. "But this is something that started hundreds of years ago and happened to come to you. Maybe you see it as luck; not me."

"We've just got to be a bit careful," Angus explained.

"You just don't want to trust me, is what you're sayin'. You want something from me, but you're comin' with an empty bucket."

They all stared at each other, locked. Clarissa crawled out from under the table, dramatically glaring at them all. "S'posed t' be nice," she said and stomped off.

Moose lifted one eyebrow and grinned. Lauchie looked at Angus. Angus gave him a nod. Lauchie looked down at the last page that he held in his hand and added it to the stack beside Moose. He noticed a slight relaxing of Moose's posture and realized that they had all lost a bit of tension.

Lauchie leaned forward on his elbow, glanced at the letter, and then at Moose. "This is just a copy," he said. "I typed it into my computer and printed it out. The original is so old that we can't risk handling it."

"The language is old and the writing is faint, so we're not sure if we got everything right," Angus added.

For a moment, no one spoke.

Moose looked down at the stacked pages but did not pick them up. "Like I said, I'm real curious, but I doubt that anyone around here would know anything about this."

"Would seem sort of mean not to let you see it now," Lauchie said.

Moose grinned and started flipping through the papers. "Sure would."

He began to read. "Say what! Is this for real?" Moose asked when he finished the first few pages.

Lauchie and Angus moved around the table to look over Moose's shoulder. "Absolutely," Angus assured him. "Pirates got him."

"Gottah be real. Nobody talks like this." Moose read on, engrossed in the story. "He makes you feel like you're right there, eh?"

"Yah," Lauchie said.

Moose continued, with Lauchie and Angus tracking the story over his shoulder. "Must've been some blow, eh?" Moose said. "Imagine going up in the riggin' in a storm like that."

"And like Lauchie said, it's not made up. This really happened to him."

"Hey, what's this? *Big native?* Native Canadian!"

Lauchie laughed. "There wasn't any Canada then, and he was from Scotland. He just got marooned here."

"Okay, we'll let it go this time."

"Come on, Moose. When you're half drowned you don't have to be politically correct."

"The key word is *big*. If that Native Canadian is big and has a nicely napped rose quartz knife, it's best to be correct."

"He was big like you." Angus offered.

"Yah, left-handed like me, too. Must've been a relative. All the men in my family are big." Moose read on. "He describes the guy's clothes. That's how my people dressed back then. See, he says the Mi'kmaw guy is better dressed. Always thought we were snappier dressers."

"Oh, man," Angus groaned. "What's 'Mi'kmaw'?"

"Mi'kmaq singular," Moose paused. "Boktusum . . . I'll have to ask Grandmother about that."

"Your grandmother knows the language?"

"She's not my grandmother," Moose explained. "Just Grandmother. Means a wise old person. She knows everything."

"We think *boktusum* means wolf, not dog, like Sea Wolf Island," Lauchie said.

Angus gave him a look, like he'd given something away. Lauchie just shrugged.

"You're right about the treasure directions," Moose said. "They're vague. What about the map?"

"We didn't bring it," Angus explained. "We made a copy, but it doesn't look like anywhere on the coast. Something's changed. The map won't help us."

"It's an amazing letter," Moose said, setting the last page down. "If you guys become millionaires with my help, you can get me some new skates, size eleven."

"Angus is awful cheap, but if we make a million, you've got it."

Moose leaned back, making the picnic bench creak. "Want to stay for supper? There's someone we could . . . maybe visit later. She might know something."

"Sure, but we'll have to call home and ask Ian to come and get us," Lauchie said, looking at Angus.

"Okay. Come and meet my mom; Dad will be in later. We'll have time to go for a swim."

"Sounds great," Lauchie said. He folded the letter and put it in his pocket as he stood up from the picnic table. They went to the house, walking easy, like three good friends. Moose held the screen door for them.

Moose's mom turned from the sink, where she was preparing greens. Her eyes had the same calm confidence as Moose's.

"Mom, meet Lauchie and Angus. You guys, meet my mom."

"So you're the hockey competition."

"We try," Lauchie said.

"Lauchie plays opposite me. He's fast."

"I'd hope so!" Moose's mom chuckled, looking at her son. "Thanks for the lobsters. I hope you'll share them with us."

"That would be nice, thanks," Angus said while Lauchie nodded.

"You'd best call home, then."

Lauchie called home first, and then called Ian, arranging to meet where he'd let them off, so they could have a bit of a bike ride before dark.

"We're goin' for a swim," Moose told his mom. To Lauchie and Angus he said, "I'll meet you guys outside. I want to change these boots."

After Angus had talked to his mother, he and Lauchie waited outside. They walked over to the table to be a bit away from the house.

"I think he's okay," Angus said.

"Yah, it's strange the letter means something different to him. We're excited about treasure and he's interested in his ancestor."

Moose slammed out the door wearing cutoffs and running shoes. "We can walk. It's just a couple of hundred yards down the road."

They walked down the gravel road together. Angus found a long stick and switched the grass at the side of the road as they walked.

"You guys are good players," Moose said.

"Yah, you too. You hit hard," Lauchie added.

"I try to play, well, try to keep learning . . . watching. I like Leetch, for defense."

"Me, too. Angus thinks I'm crazy. Who you like for baseball?"

"Cleveland Native Americans."

Lauchie looked at Moose. Moose grinned, cocked his head, and shrugged. "Well, you asked."

"I hear you, Moose."

Angus looked at Moose. "Lauchie said that you're doing oysters."

"Yah. The heavy equipment—the dozer and all—are the real business, but we want to keep the grounds. It's like a family thing, and everyone helps out with it. Keeps me busy, but it's good work. I like bein' on the water in the early mornin'."

"Me, too," Lauchie said. "My mom didn't want me to fish. She was afraid I'd like it too much, afraid I'd quit school."

"Yah. I got a bit of that," Moose said. "How'd you handle it?"

"I rigged up a school project about lobster counts and stuff, and that tipped the scales for me." Lauchie looked at Moose. "What'd you do?"

"First off, my dad's desperate for help. Second, I claimed native traditions. Even a mom can't argue with that."

"Listen up, Lauchie," Angus said. "This guy can teach you something."

"Mom negotiations make great political training." Moose pointed to a beaten track through the weeds. "If we follow this, it'll take us down to a good pool in the river."

Moose went first, down a steep path that led off into the woods. Angus followed close behind him. "Hey, Moose, you like computer games?"

"You kiddin'? I'm acing Zydag IV."

"There's a four now? I didn't know that."

"Yah, it's better; it's got some twists. You can try it when we get back to the house."

They arrived at the river. Elsewhere it was fast, wide, and shallow, but here it narrowed. A raised rib of water-smoothed bedrock created a small waterfall about four feet high, and the turbulence of the fall had carved out a deep, round pool. Ash and red maples hung over the banks, and the high afternoon sun filtered through the leaves, making dappled golden patches on the bottom and shimmering reflections on the surface. As they approached, they saw a single big brook trout hovering just off a deep cut in the bank of the pool. He was facing into the current but suddenly sped down stream in a blur of speed.

"That's Tommy Trout. We catch-proofed him."

"You what?" Angus asked.

"We caught him three times with barbless hooks and different kinds of tackle. We kept letting him go. Now he's too smart to be caught. We want to see how big and old he'll get."

"Two guys could catch him," Lauchie boasted.

"Not my trout," Moose said.

Lauchie explained his idea. "One guy puts a line with live bait, like a worm, maybe. The other guy brings a lure that looks like a little fish up to the bait; as though it's gonnah eat it. The trout will either take the bait or, more likely, the little fish."

"Lauchie, you're a real piece of work," Angus said.

"Leave my fish alone," Moose added.

"Sure. I'd like to see how he does, too," Lauchie agreed. "I want to study ocean fish."

"I want to swim!" Angus yelled as he dove in a flash of brilliant red boxers, followed by the others.

Lauchie dove deep and followed the bottom. He could see his own shadow, like a dark smudge, to his right. Pebbles on the bottom looked like blurry gold and amber gems. He stayed under as long as he could stand it, turned and came up under the falls. He grabbed a worn crack in the rock, and hung there, pummeled by the cascading water, then let go to ride the current. "Moose, this is the best pool!" he yelled.

Moose was floating on his back, only stroking enough to stay in a big swirling eddy. "Yah, low upkeep, no chlorine, and not too crowded."

They walked back to the house feeling cooler and refreshed by the swim. Though Moose's house was similar to Lauchie's, the original building had been extended at the back to allow a larger kitchen, and the driveway had been widened and extended for heavy equipment like the dozer. They went into the kitchen. Clarissa was setting the table, making each setting a unique combination of knives, forks, and spoons. Moose's mother stood by the stove, where a huge pot of water was just beginning to boil.

"Moose, just in time. Your dad's due any time now. Would you do the lobsters, please?"

Clarissa patiently stood behind Moose with a live lobster until it hooked onto his T-shirt. Moose began an elaborate act: "Save me! It's getting me!" while Clarissa jumped up and down, cheering for the lobster. He began windmilling his arms and staggering backward shouting, "Help! It's Crusher Claw! He's dragging me away. . . ." He backed up, leaning backward until he was over the stove and the hot steam, so that the lobster fell into the pot, then he turned and looked at the pot. "That's not enough for me. What I need is some little sister stew." Clarissa shrieked and ran out giggling.

Lauchie heard the growl of a big truck engine and the heavy crunch of driveway gravel. Moose's mom looked up from the stove. "There's your dad. Moose, take these boys to get washed up. Food'll be ready in a minute."

Moose's dad was like a Moose copy, a bit heavier and just as tall. As they ate, Lauchie wondered why they had ever hesitated to talk to Moose. The kitchen they were eating in was similar to his own. The lobsters were accompanied by the same kind of greens from the garden, and the potatoes were Cape Breton blues. Moose and Angus were having an animated discussion about Zydag IV. Moose's dad looked at Lauchie. "You're Ian's neighbor. I've seen you at the games."

"Yes."

"Say hello for me. We did some work together a few years ago. He's a good man."

"He's been good to me."

Moose's dad nodded, then looked around the table. "These lobsters are a fine treat. Thank you, boys."

"I want to save two for Grandmother," Moose said. "Lauchie and Angus have some questions for her about the old days. I would like to take them to visit."

"*Treasure,*" Clarissa whispered.

"Clarissa! This stuff is real private. Little sisters shouldn't have such big ears."

Moose's dad looked thoughtfully at Moose. "I'm not askin'," he said.

After supper, Moose's mom wrapped two lobsters in a clean dishtowel. "Say hello for me. Tell her that old Ben needs more of whatever she gives him for his arthritis. If you can bring it back, I'll take it to him."

"Sure, Mom," Moose grinned at Lauchie and Angus. "Grandmother's super tea."

As Lauchie and Angus said their thanks and good-byes, Moose herded them toward the door.

Clarissa scampered around Moose and ran toward Lauchie. She was scrunched down and grimacing, with her hands in claw shapes, at shoulder height. "Crusher Claw's going to get you!"

Lauchie quickly caught her up and swung her above his head. "I'm a crusher claw catcher—that's what I do. I'm a crusher claw catcher, and now I've caught you."

Clarissa giggled, looking down at him. "Will you come back again to visit?"

"Yes."

8

GRANDMOTHER

Moose got his bike, and together they rode down the road. Soon they came to a widening that formed a turnaround at the end of the road. The area was mostly wooded, with a mixture of birch, ash, and pine. A short graveled drive led to a house.

Grandmother must have heard their voices, because she met them at the door. She was a tiny lady who made quick, almost birdlike gestures. She poked Moose in the ribs. "Where have you been? You are neglectful of this old one."

"Sorry, Grandmother. I have brought friends to meet you."

"Then come in. We'll have tea."

Grandmother's kitchen had an old and simple look. The cupboards were pine that had aged to a deep gold. Over the enamel sink, a west-facing window caught the sun's lowering rays, which cast golden beams on the pine table. The floor was raw wood, so deeply worn by traffic and scrubbing that knots stood out as bumps.

There was a trace of sweet grass in the air, mixed with scents of herbs that hung in bunches from the rafters, the faint, clean tang of homemade soap, and the toasty aroma of scorched birch bark.

"We've eaten, Grandmother," Moose said, "but we brought you some fresh cooked lobster."

She smelled them saying, "Mmm. West shore."

"You can tell just like that?" Angus asked.

Grandmother laughed, giving Angus a poke. "No, dear," she said. "I can tell because you both play hockey for that side."

"You go to the games?"

"Of course. One never knows when Little Moose might need some special coaching."

She made tea and steamed some docks, which were like wild spinach, and made everyone taste them; then she listened to their story while she enjoyed the lobster and they all drank tea.

When they had wound down with their explanations, Grandmother sat quietly for a moment, and then began to speak in a slightly different way, as though each word were chosen with care.

"My grandmother taught me all the old stories that she knew. Now we can write them down—that was not always so. Stories are like a tricky person. One must watch them very carefully, or they will become something else. My grandmother couldn't write and had no desire to; she taught me in the old way. It was not enough to know the story. One must know it exactly, so that the story could not change. This is a great responsibility, because if a storyteller lets a few words change, here and there, then a bit of Mi'kmaq history might be lost forever. So I learned the old way." She sighed and took a sip of her tea.

"It is the Mi'kmaq way to expect all people to do their best. That's why competitions are so silly— except hockey, of course. We are not perfect. We do our best, but sometimes a story gets away. It would be wrong to change a story, but one might wonder, 'Just what did this mean?'"

Grandmother paused, and sipped more tea. "I won't tell you any stories today. They are about other things. But I will tell you about two names that I recall that I think might have been the same man, and may have been that doctor. Perhaps as they got to know him better, he became like another man. It is often like that, when you learn to know someone."

Grandmother looked at Lauchie then continued: "I don't remember a story, but I remember the name 'Animal Face.' The People were very honest. If they had never, or rarely, seen a European, and he had a big beard, they might call him Animal Face. They wouldn't do this to be nasty. It would just seem that he had a furry face. What is, is. The name might refer to any very early arrival to our land. Sixteen thirty-two is not that early for the mainland. But perhaps, on this island . . ." Grandmother leaned back in her chair, making an offhand gesture.

"What's the other name?" Angus asked.

"I remember hearing a phrase that would translate to 'healer who knew no healing.' It makes me wonder: If a man came who could do some healing and set bones but knew no Mi'kmaq cures or rituals, might not that be what they would call him?" Grandmother sat back, and sipped her tea.

"What's *boktusum* mean?" Moose asked.

"It means *wolf*, Moose," Grandmother said with a stern look. "You should know more of the simple words."

"Have you ever heard of 'Little Sea Wolf Island?'" Angus asked her.

"No, but it was probably near Sea Wolf Island."

"But there's no other island near there," Lauchie said.

"Remember, the earth is a living thing. It must renew itself. It is always changing—usually very slowly, because it is so big, and because it must do it just right. Rivers move; shores move back, then forward."

"What about the emerald?" Lauchie asked. "Wouldn't that be kind of famous?"

"Perhaps it was just accepted as a gift. You must realize," Grandmother added with a twinkle in her eye, "that the Mi'kmaq did not have the same obsession with bigness that is so common today. Too often bigger meant heavier to carry, or tougher to chew, or just plain wasteful.

"The reason for stories is to tell us who we are and how we should act. I have no facts for you, young man, but I have some advice," she said, giving Lauchie a poke. "It is a grandmother's job to give advice. If what you want is good and you search with an open heart, then the earth and the sea may help you. This letter is the sea's gift to you. If you search thinking of profit, then I think you will have no success.

"Now," said Grandmother, "here is my advice. I can't tell you just how a Mi'kmaw would do this, but I can tell you some things that will help." She made a half-poking gesture toward Lauchie.

"The sea gave you this gift near the wharf, so I'd think that you would begin there. Choose a quiet day at the wharf, a Sunday morning, perhaps. Eat a very light supper the night before and the next morning wash well without scented soap, so that the flies won't distract you. Just have a little tea for breakfast. It is not natural to search or hunt when one has no need. Take a blanket to sit on and some water to drink. Find a high place that overlooks the area, but don't sit where you *think* you should; wander around until you find a place that feels good, and just sit there quietly. Think of yourself as Nature's guest and be open to the guidance of your host on how you should act." She sipped her tea.

"Let yourself imagine the land changing over the years. Don't try to think hard. If your mind wanders to a cloud or a tree, that is all right, but pull your thoughts gently back to your purpose, like a quiet conversation with the land and the sea. Think of the old letter as a friend—not the words of the letter, but the thing itself. It came to you. Let it help you. You may be surprised at how your time stills while other time moves on and how good that will feel."

If anyone else had said this, at any other time, Lauchie would have laughed, but he felt a powerful conviction in Grandmother's words.

"Picture how the land may have changed," Grandmother repeated. "Watch it in your mind. If something is there and you are worthy to find it, I think you might see land where once there was sea, and sea where once there was land."

They all sat quietly for a few moments. Grandmother regarded Lauchie over the rim of her teacup; it was a look of joyful anticipation. Moose looked completely relaxed. He smiled and glanced at Lauchie. Lauchie gave a slight nod as though to say, "Yes, Moose, I get it." Angus glanced about, looking just a little uncertain.

It was getting late. Moose was going to stay to visit. Lauchie and Angus left, thanking Moose and Grandmother and promising to let them know what happened. As they left, Grandmother cautioned Lauchie, "This sign came to you, a gift of the sea. You must think on it alone."

As they rode down the drive, they heard Grandmother laugh about something with Moose. It was a gentle, clear sound that hung in the air like a bell.

It was well before dark, and Angus and Lauchie

wanted to ride as far as possible before meeting Ian. "Don't you dare say anything about this to anyone," Lauchie threatened, already panting as they got their bikes up to speed.

"You mean the hokum?" Angus teased.

"All of it," Lauchie said firmly. "But I'm not so sure that it's hokum," he added, positive that it was not, and feeling both excited and amazed at this new and strange notion.

9

SITTING ON TREASURE

On Sunday morning, Lauchie was honest but vague in the note that he left for his mother:

> *Mom,*
> *Going to the wharf.*
> *I may be gone quite a while.*
> *Lauchie*

He left it to his mom to assume that he'd eaten breakfast; she had been concerned enough when he'd made a supper of salad greens the night before. He was going to follow Grandmother's directions, but he felt uncomfortable about defending the logic of his actions.

Dog seemed to know that this was not a working day. He went through his morning ritual of thrusting his paws forward to stretch his back, a position much like his "let's play" gesture, then vigorously shook his head and stretched his jaws in a human-like yawn. His preparation complete, he bounded to Lauchie.

Free of the normal rush to get out to sea, Lauchie rode his bike slowly down to the wharf. The morning air was chill and the scent from the fields intense. Spider webs glittered faint and elusive with drops of dew, and the big white flowers of Queen Anne's lace glowed dimly in the darkness of the tall grass. Dog loped just ahead, a shadow against the tall weeds along the shoulder of the road.

The wharf was deserted, and a light chop washed against the breakwater. The boats seemed to murmur to one another, making rubbing and bumping sounds.

He imagined with a shiver what it would feel like to have his own boat. What would he call her? She'd be white, that was for sure, deep-keeled and agile, and when he stood, brace-legged in a stiff breeze, he would feel that keel like the nerves in his own backbone. She needn't be big, he thought, just a good Cape Islander that he could trust in a breeze.

He left his bike behind Ian's trap shed and began climbing the big bald hill that overlooked the harbor to the west and Margaree Island to the north. As he climbed, he looked back down on the summer-dried marsh behind the harbor. It looked like a big oval bowl, filled with luminous gray fog that was trapped in the low ground. He climbed until he'd reached the highest point, which was the leading edge of the cliffs.

Following Grandmother's advice, he ambled around the area, not really knowing what he was trying to sense. But he always seemed to end up standing right above the crow's nest that gave the tiny cove its name. Partway down the cliff, a large rock protruded, and crows nested there every year. He decided to sit there, above the nest.

Lauchie unfolded and spread his blanket. At this height, the grass was short and the wind had dried any dew that might have been there. He put down his water bottle and stood looking all about him, feeling uncertain just how to go about this.

To the north, below him, the cliff dropped away into the Crow's Nest Cove. On his left a boulder-strewn steep slope faced west over the harbor and down the coast, and between the two an almost-cliff of loose scree faced out over the Marsh Point Grounds. To his right the coast ran northeast, toward Donk's Mountain, which sloped steeply to the sea.

The sun rose in a rush, as though it had been gathering strength behind the mountain, waiting to pounce into the morning sky. The first rays hit well clear of the shore, lighting the cliffs on the island and bringing them into sudden sharp focus. Then the line of light rolled over the sea toward the shore, bringing the somber waves into a new, sparkling world.

The grounds, where they fished, came into view, so clear from that height. The rocks and weeds of the lobsters' habitat showed as purple blotches against the turquoise-green background of sand bottom that surrounded them. The sun caught the swamp, and Lauchie watched the gray fog flash to white, quickly warming, sending tentacles spiraling skyward to dissipate in the breeze above.

As Lauchie settled on his blanket, Dog gave his equivalent of a shrug and loped off along the cliff's edge.

At first Lauchie thought about everything but what he'd come for. His thoughts drifted to Moose; how different he was with his family and how far he was from the image that he and Angus had created. He thought about Grandmother, and the special clear way that she seemed to speak, and then he realized that it was not a way of speaking but a sureness of absolute belief. She was someone who said, "What is, is." He held that phrase in his mind like a pleasant taste, and liked it. He thought about fishing and how he loved it.

Now with each thought he began directing his mind back to the problem, until it finally seemed to be a constant awareness. As he looked about, he gradually began seeing things with less internal comment; simply enjoying and accepting what he saw.

His breathing had slowed to match the languid pulse of the surf below, and he sensed its resonance in the earth beneath him. He closed his eyes. It seemed as though the subtle sounds of surge and retreat defined the shape of rocks and beach, invisible from where he sat. The ground was heated by the strengthening sun, and the earthy smells of dawn changed to scents of warming grass and blueberry blossoms.

Without really thinking about it, he felt lighter and relaxed. Time was neither a thought nor a consideration. He opened his eyes and looked around. He watched a diving gull wheel over his head. It was so much slighter than the big sea gulls, with swallow-like tapered wings. It seemed to spin in the air, then went into its dive, hard to track in its eye-blurring speed. It was diving over the swamp and pulled out at the last second, buzzing the wharf on its way out to sea.

Lauchie was so disappointed at not seeing its typical plunge that he imagined it. He imagined the gull plummeting into . . . a sea pond filled with fish.

And then he knew.

He knew that in the 1600s there was a sea pond where the summer-dried swamp was now. He knew that the canyon-like gully that ran parallel to the sea along the road once held more than the trickle it now did, that the break in the cliffs just a few hundred feet east of him was not without cause. It had been cut by a strong outward flow of water that, for some reason, was now only a trickle. He knew that he was sitting on Little Sea Wolf Island.

Lauchie shivered with excitement, then with fear, wondering if he was just wanting it to be so. Yet the more he looked down at the swamp, the more convinced he became.

He began scanning the new land, or, more accurately, the old one, in his mind. He imagined the virgin forest growing almost to the beach. The road down to the wharf, built up with loads of gravel every spring for as long as anyone could remember, was, even now, only a few feet above sea level. It was easy to see it as a shallow curve of gravel and sand almost linking the island to the land. Lauchie felt thirsty and noticed that his water was sitting out in the sun, then realized that he'd been there much longer than he'd thought. He rinsed his mouth and poured the rest around a stunted blueberry bush.

As he started to refold his blanket, Dog dashed over the brow, grabbing a corner of it for a tug of war. His eyes had the gleam of recent adventure. "Wish you could tell me about it," Lauchie commented as he rescued the blanket. They set off down the hill together.

Lauchie felt as though he now had knowledge that no one else had. He knew what the shore was like in 1632. This new vision felt like a gift, and it made him feel even closer to the land and sea around him. He was walking down a steep, bald-looking hill, but he was also walking down a hill of virgin pine and oak. The young doctor of so long ago seemed more real and believable.

Mary seemed to know that Lauchie hadn't eaten. She made him a monster snack and didn't press him about what he'd been up to. He looked up with a grin. "Still thinking, Mom. When I've got it solid, I'll tell you."

"I just don't want to see you obsessed with this treasure stuff. I spoke to a gentleman at the Halifax Museum. He said that he has a summer place by

Red River and he'd like to see the letter the next time that he's out here."

"Okay, but I want to talk to him first."

"Of course. What's happening with your lobster-count project? I don't hear much about that anymore."

"It's happening. Angus and I each keep a little notebook under the bow decks." He made a quick duck as she tried to ruffle his hair. He left to call Angus saying, "You're still my main man, Mom." This got him a severe hair ruffling and laughter that helped to break the spell. He could talk to Angus now without blurting out stuff that he'd never be able to explain.

Angus answered the phone, not bothering to check who it was. "Yah, whaddah ya want, hot shot?"

"Hello," Lauchie said, pitching his voice, "this is the Inverness Bank calling. Could I speak with your mommy, please?"

"Cut it out, Lauchie."

"What's wrong with you?"

"I don't like bein' left out, is all," Angus said.

"We decided to do it this way, like Grandmother said, and you agreed. Come on—loosen up. I've got pretty good news."

"You know where it is?"

"Well, where it *should* be," Lauchie said, "or at least where it *could* be."

"So where is it?"

"Well, it's not for sure. Come on over and I'll show you what I figured out. Bring that little half-sized miner's pick. Maybe we can do some exploring."

Angus was too excited to stay grouchy for long. "Yah, well, I'll be over—in a while—maybe."

Five minutes later he arrived. "So how was the magic quest?"

"It wasn't a big deal. It wasn't just ordinary, either. Something happened out there, like my thinking got helped a bit. That's all."

Angus looked a bit hurt. "Hey, you're not turning into some kind of weirdo, are you?"

"Look," Lauchie said, "I just thought we should take Grandmother's advice. And it sort of worked."

"Yah, well, I thought we were in this together."

"Come on, Angus. I just tried something that might help."

"So we gonnah cut the Moose in on it now?"

"No way. It's like Moose said, this is our quest. But I gottah say, I liked Moose."

"Me, too," Angus admitted. "We're like the guys in all those old movies. They go looking for gold, then shoot each other when they find it."

"Nah. I don't think it's about gold so much. It's our adventure."

"Okay, okay. So what did you find out?"

As far as the present geography was concerned, Lauchie and Angus had an advantage. They'd grown up roaming the land and watching the sea. They quickly sketched a map marking deep holes and rock bars. If they'd wanted to, they could have marked depths.

With their copy of the doctor's map to one side, Lauchie started drawing a new map, and as he worked and explained each item, his ideas were punctuated by Angus saying, "Yah" and "Of course" and "Why didn't we see that?"

"We didn't see it because all our lives we saw the way it is now," Lauchie said.

It all seemed so obvious to Lauchie, as though he'd only been encouraged to think things out. He said nothing about the diving gull.

"So the break in the cliffs," he continued, "it's got to be for a reason. Something made a cut over a hundred feet. Maybe thousands of years ago there was a waterfall there, before the sea pond, when all the land was still higher."

"Yah," Angus said, "and that long canyon-like valley runs parallel to the sea and ends at the marsh. There's just a little trickle down there now, but it cut that huge gash in the earth all along the Marsh Road. Maybe the creek that flows by Donk's Mountain used to go that way."

"No, I don't think so," Lauchie said. "That valley is bigger, older. What if there were two creeks in that big valley, one going to the sea pond, and then they joined, and most of the sea pond creek drained off into Donk's?"

Angus began bouncing his pencil on the sea pond area. "Okay, we've got a strong creek coming into the area where the marsh is now. Way, way back in time, maybe where the wharf is was hard bedrock, so the creek cuts through the cliffs in two places."

"Yah, there's still that big rock in the harbor. Maybe that was part of it."

"Sure," Angus said. "And over the years the sea-ward side becomes the main channel, leaving an island that's joined by a shallow spit where the wharf is now."

"Maybe it was just a high-tide island."

"Yah, and when the creek got smaller, it would no longer flush out the pond. It would gradually fill up with muck."

"And the loot," Lauchie said, "is at the highest point of the island, behind a big square rock that might have disappeared into the sea, or was broken up by frost, because I didn't see it up there."

"It's gottah be there," Angus said. "Maybe it's buried, or under a rock pile."

"Well, let's go look. But let's be real quiet and cool about this."

"Yah," Angus agreed. "We don't want anybody laughing at us."

"Right. We'll look carefully and think it through. Let's go."

10

THE SEARCH

Lauchie and Angus grabbed their bikes and rode to Ian's barn. They borrowed a shovel and crowbar, adding them to Angus's small pick. With the tools across their handlebars and Dog loping ahead, they headed for the harbor.

They rode down the gravel lane to the harbor and into the turnaround, followed by a ribbon of dust. The wharf was deserted, the boats rocking gently against their bumpers. They stashed their bikes behind Ian's shed.

In the shimmering heat of the day the high hill looked like a mountain. The tools felt awkward and heavy. Even Dog seemed subdued, omitting his normal side trips.

"There be treasure yonder, me hearties," Angus growled, as they began their climb, using the tools like walking sticks. They paused to rest halfway up, looking down at what they now called the lagoon.

Their theory was easier to imagine on a map at home. Here it looked like a hot, dried-up swamp. The rising hill ahead of them looked too familiar and normal to be a place where treasure would be found.

They crested the hill, dropped the heavy tools on a low-spread rock pile, and headed for the cliff edge, scooping up strawberries as they went.

The sea had a nice roll now, giving each wave crest fine lines of broken white water. The high sun sparkled and glinted off the sea, and the buoys left streaky wake lines on the backs of the passing waves.

"Okay," Lauchie said, pointing about, "there's Jonathan's Grounds to the southwest, then Shag Rock Grounds. Imagine the point thrusting way out toward the island. Imagine the island a bit longer and wider, the cliffs closer, and this point we're on extending north and nor'west out over the Marsh Point Grounds toward the island."

"Yah," Angus agreed, "and the south shore maybe a couple of hundred feet farther out, Donk's Mountain reaching well into the channel. Add the entrance to the lagoon and we've got just what the ship's doctor described."

"Imagine how it must have looked then," Lauchie said. "There'd be big trees right to the cliff tops, making everything look higher and wilder. I bet the wind was at its worst just before Donk's Mountain."

"Right, that's where the mast would let go. She'd catch the rocks below us but farther out, and the storm would break her up and swing her in near where the harbor is now."

"Let's get on with it."

They decided to walk a grid back and forth across the hilltop. A big rock could become buried in time on a hillside, but it was not likely to happen on *top* of a hill. Since the letter described a big rock, visible even in the forest, it should still be there. It could have been buried in a rock pile, but they could see no large rock piles, which added to their fears that the land where the big rock rested had long ago fallen into the sea. They walked about twenty feet apart, back and forth across the highest point, turning when the ground began to slope down. The area was less than an acre, and after about two hours they had thoroughly covered it, finding nothing more interesting than a fantastic patch of strawberries. Tired and frustrated, they returned to the cliff edge and sat eating berries and looking out over the sea.

"Embarrassing," Angus complained, "wandering around a field on a hot day."

"It's here somewhere," Lauchie said. "I just know it."

Angus was holding his berries in his open left hand, eating them one at a time. Dog eased up beside him, made a sudden jab at his hand, scarfed up most of the berries, and quickly jumped back out of reach.

"You stupid thief!" Angus yelled. "Dogs don't eat berries."

Dog sat with his lolling-tongued grin and a bright red smear on the end of his nose.

"He can't help it," Lauchie explained, laughing at them both. "If you eat it, it's food. He'll try to rip you off even if he doesn't like it."

Dog watched them both with gleeful eyes as his tongue flicked out to clean the juice from his nose. Then, with a cross-eyed look, he sneezed and flopped down.

Lauchie was throwing pebbles at a big square flagstone that had slid partway down the scree slope. He watched them bounce, sometimes all the way to the water. The slope wasn't a cliff like the Crow's Nest to their right, but it was steep and covered with loose shale that would send you sliding if you set foot on it. The sea that was pounding into boulders at the foot of the slope was more than a hundred feet below them.

Angus pointed at the square, flat rock. "If we could get to that big sucker, give it a nudge, it would make some splash."

"What if it wouldn't move?" Lauchie suggested, a thought beginning to grow. "What if it wasn't a flat slab, but a square rock, sunk into the hillside?"

"Nah, it's a big flat flag. . . . I think."

"Well, let's say it's the rock in the letter. How do we get the treasure? Did the stuff stay under it as it slid down the slope, or get left behind, or go over the cliff?"

Angus began to accept the idea. "It would probably have happened in the spring, when the clay was saturated. We should check it out."

They thought no more about the unlikelihood of it being the right rock. It was their only hope of keeping the search alive, and their spirits improved. They tried to imagine the rock's journey from a decaying hilltop; sliding in the soupy muck as the spring frost came out. The big question was whether the treasure was still behind the rock, or had it flowed around the rock, immersed in liquefied mud? The rock had probably moved in the last few years, from the top of the hill.

"We can get to it with ropes," Angus suggested.

"Yah, but we'll be exposed out there."

"It'll be afternoons," Angus said. "After fishin', so no boats will be out. If tourists come by, we'll just say we're looking for treasure. They'll figure we're crazy."

"We could make a camouflage net out of an old bait net to cover the dig."

"Nah," Angus said, "we can just put some old gray planks over it, and some dry mud."

Their plan worked out at last, they knew that they first needed to bring some iron bars to drive into the ground to hold ropes, and some rope to support them on the slope. They would dig around the rock before they committed to carrying boards up the hill.

"It's too late to start today," Angus said.

"Yah, tomorrow we start. From here on, we say nothing about it to anyone."

They hid the tools in a blackberry patch so that they wouldn't have to carry them up again and headed for home, not certain but at least with a sense of hope.

Dog gave Angus a nudge as they started down the hill. "Sure, sure, no hard feelings, you old thief," Angus told him, then he looked around. "It looks too normal here."

"Okay, so imagine that we were standing right here, but it isn't open field and sun. Imagine that we're in virgin woods—never been cut. There's big thick-trunked oaks and pines, a hundred feet tall. The sea sounds far away. You can smell cinnamon ferns. We climb to the top of this hill and see a big old flat-topped boulder all covered with wet, green moss. Golden beams streak through the branches above us and make splotches of light on the big rock. . . ."

"Whoa, Lauchie, you're drifting a bit far off shore there. But, yah, that's more like it—could be treasure there all right."

"Well, that's what it was like back then."

They left the steepness of the hill and walked toward the wharf, retrieved their bikes from behind Ian's trap shed, and started home. Dog loped beside them. They were almost home when an unfamiliar pickup, traveling in the opposite direction, passed them. Lauchie could hear the truck slowing and then stopping. He turned his head to see it reversing. They stopped and waited for the truck to get back to them. Lauchie could see a couple of chainsaws in the back, gas tanks and chain-oil containers, with an old piece of bait net thrown on top to hold it all down. The passenger door swung open and Moose jumped to the road. He was wearing gray-striped engineer's coveralls and a beaten-up welder's cap with giant multi-colored spots on it.

Lauchie let his bike rest in the weeds off the shoulder, and nodded to Moose's dad, who was at the wheel. "Moose, what are you doin' way over here?"

"Gottah go where the work is. I didn't know you were this close by. Dad's just starting a woods-road contract, about four miles down the road. We're cuttin' the pulp and firewood first, then we'll gravel over the brush."

Lauchie looked at Moose's dad. "Can you stop in for a snack?"

"I'd like to, but I've got some chores and errands to do yet today."

"I could ask my mom if you can stay over," Lauchie said. "You could come out in the boat in the morning."

Moose looked at his dad.

His dad nodded. "In the morning, I'll be hauling some gravel over our way. You could skip the oysters for a day. They'll be fine. Will you be ready to do some serious cuttin' by one tomorrow?"

Moose looked at Lauchie, got a nod, looked back at his dad. "Yah, sure," he said, grinning, "if the fishing isn't too tiring."

Lauchie and Angus put their bikes in the back and crawled onto the bed of the truck. Moose joined them. Dog stood on the shoulder with his tongue hanging to the side wearing a very attentive look. As soon as he saw the truck start to make a U-turn, he took off toward home. Moose's dad saw him, quickly completed his turn, and sped up. The road was deserted, and he kept the truck behind and safely away from Dog. Lauchie, Angus, and Moose were standing up, leaning on the cab, cheering Dog on. He was running all out, stretched low to the ground. They neared Ian's place, where the road was much higher than the adjacent field. Dog bounded into the air, cleared Ian's fence, and cut a diagonal across the field. "He's cheating!" Moose yelled.

Lauchie laughed. "Dog rules."

"Well, I guess my dad doesn't need directions to your house now."

The truck drove up Lauchie's driveway. Dog stood in the middle of the drive, chest heaving and tongue hanging out. Angus pointed at him. "He's definitely laughing at us."

Lauchie jumped off the truck while it was still rolling and ran into the house.

"Lauchie," Mary called out, "don't slam the door." One of her clients was just leaving.

"Mom, Moose is here—can he stay for supper? Stay over?"

"Lauchie, slow down. Yes, Maurice can stay over. I haven't any fresh hockey sticks, though."

Lauchie's face flushed. "Mom, don't you dare!" He ran out, letting the door slam, and then slowed to a more dignified walk, over to the truck. "It's cool."

Moose's dad was still sitting in the truck, which he'd turned around. He eased it slowly forward, nodded to Lauchie, looked at Moose. "Have a good time. See you round one tomorrow."

"Come on in and meet my mom."

They went up the porch steps together. As Lauchie reached ahead to open the door, his mom approached from the inside. "Lauchie, if you slam that door again, you'll be roadkill. Hi, Maurice. I've been hearing about you from Lauchie."

"Everyone calls me Moose. Not bad, I hope—what you hear."

"Hmm," Mary set her tea on the kitchen table and sat down, smiling at Moose. "Will you have supper with us, and stay over?"

"Yes, thank you."

Angus and Lauchie were already grabbing chairs.

"I was going to cook some fresh herring for supper, but it won't be ready for a while. Do you like herring?"

"Herring? Yah, love 'em."

"Lauchie, there's a big bottle of ginger ale in the fridge. Why don't you put that out, and some glasses and ice. Angus, are you going to stay for supper?"

"Sure, thanks."

Lauchie started rummaging in the freezer. "Hey, super chocolate ice—"

"Lauchie, you're eating soon. Forget the ice cream. . . . Are you having a nice summer, Moose?"

"Keepin' busy—working with my dad, looking after the oysters."

"Are you the same age as Lauchie and Angus?"

Moose shrugged, looking at Lauchie. "Just turned fifteen."

"Angus and I are fourteen," Lauchie said. "Mom didn't want me to fish this year."

"Mine, neither," Moose said.

Mary looked up. "So what scheme did you cook up?"

Moose grinned. "Native traditions, keeping the oyster grounds; plus my dad needs the help. I heard about Lauchie's deal—tricky."

"Hey, we're doin' it, for real. It's a valuable project."

"I believe you," Mary said. "And when I imagine you lying around the house all summer, I'm glad to be rid of you."

"Now you say that!" Lauchie said.

"Well, I do worry, you know, and I don't know how I'll ever get enough berries picked."

Lauchie scowled at his mom, but no one seemed to notice.

"Getting any mackerel?" Moose asked.

"Not yet," Lauchie said. "On this side of the island they seem to come later in the season."

"With the black fish," Angus added.

"Lauchie, would you please take out the compost and cut me some salad greens? Cut some chard, too, if there's enough for a meal."

"Yah, sure." Lauchie took the covered crock of vegetable scraps from the kitchen counter. "Just take a minute."

Angus grabbed a paring knife and a colander, and they all left for the garden.

The garden was behind the barn on the southeast side, protected from the sea winds from the north and northwest. It was about eighty feet by eighty feet, with a high chicken-wire fence to keep out the deer and rabbits. The fence at the north side was covered with the tentacles of young scarlet runner beans that had just begun to blossom. A wooden gate allowed entry at the northwest corner and the compost was in a log crib in the opposite corner. The east and west fences were lined with currant bushes and raspberry canes. The rest of the garden was laid out in raised beds formed by logs set into the ground. One bed was a mixture of salad greens that Lauchie began to choose from. "Angus, go pull us some scallions, over there. They're tiny but good."

Moose went to another bed and thinned some carrots, keeping the thinnings for the salad. "Nice garden," he said.

"Yah, Mom's a good gardener. She makes me do the heavy stuff, but she works at it the most."

"No potatoes, no turnips?"

"Nah. We trade off with Ian. He does the potatoes, turnips, and corn; we do the exotic stuff. Close the gate. I'll run this stuff back to the house."

When Lauchie came out again, Moose and Angus were sitting on the ground under the big apple tree. It was southwest of the house, on the other side of the driveway and in front of the old barn. Lauchie maintained a circle of lawn around and under the tree because it was a shady place to sit. Moose picked up a short stick, showed it to Dog, and threw it. Dog watched the stick's end-over-end arc far out into the field, and then sat, watching Lauchie approach.

"Hey, you never taught him to fetch," Moose said to Lauchie.

"He figures it's your stick, so you can go chase it."

Angus pointed out into the field. "Dog! Rabbit!" Dog raised his head for the slightest of sniffs, gave Angus a glance then lay down, lowering his head to rest on his paws.

"Nice view here. There's the famous island, Margaree . . . Sea Wolf . . . Boktusum."

"See the southwest end, where the whitewater's breaking? I found the old crock just out from there. We were tied up to the bait net."

"Hate to pry, but are you having any luck with the treasure?"

"Still trying. What Grandmother said helped. She made me think about a lot of stuff—not just about the treasure."

"Yah, she seems to do that for some people. I'm glad that I introduced you."

"I think Lauchie's going all native," Angus said.

"No way," Moose said. "I'm all native. You're all Scots, should be speakin' the Gaelic, dressin' funny, and playin' those horrible pipes."

"I hear you," Lauchie said. He lay back on the lawn, looking up into the shadowed depth of the big apple tree. "When we were kids, about ten, Angus and I used to climb this tree on really windy days. We'd hang on and look over the edge of a branch so that we couldn't see any land—just the stormy sea. We'd pretend that we were in a ship's rigging. So one windy day we really got into it. We had pieces of lobster-trap rope and cloth and stuff up there. We made a Jolly Roger flag and hung it way up high. Angus gets this idea that we should have real sails, so I go get the sheets off my bed. Mom's busy with a customer, doesn't notice."

Angus poked Lauchie's shoulder, taking over. "Lauchie comes out with the sheets and some old bailing twine. He's got the bread knife to cut the string. It's tucked under his belt, like a pirate. He's got an old tie wrapped around his head, and one for me. He climbs back up in the tree, and we tie the sheets to the limbs, like sails."

Lauchie was still lying down, listening to Angus. He sat up, laughing. "It's late October, the tree's bare, and there's about a thirty-mile-an-hour wind. Our sails are snapping and popping in the gusts, and a dark squall is coming across the sea. It rushes across the fields, comin' right at us. The squall hits us, ice-cold and wet, and then it just keeps on going over the barn, the mountain. We don't care. The rain's like salt spray. We're totally out of control. Angus and I are bouncing on one branch and hangin' on to another. We're yelling out dumb stuff like, 'Reef the mains'l, me hearties.' We're having such fun, it never occurs to us that my mom's gonnah freak out when she sees us."

Moose lay on the lawn, resting on one elbow, looking from Lauchie to Angus as their story progressed. "You got caught?"

Angus looked at Lauchie, then Moose. "It was inevitable. Some lady from town comes for a haircut. She turns up the driveway, sees us, and almost goes in the ditch; slams her car door and goes running into the house."

"My mom and this lady and another neighbor wearing a dumb-looking haircut smock all come running out of the house."

"Lauchie's mom is going nutsie-kaboogoo."

Lauchie looked intently at Moose. "She's really mad, but what's worse is she's embarrassed, too, 'cause her kid's such an idiot. So she's yelling at us to get down out of the tree, 'cause we're gonnah kill ourselves, 'cause we're wet, 'cause we're gonnah get sick, 'cause we're out of our minds."

"But the sheets are still in the tree," Angus said, flopping on his back, laughing.

Lauchie takes over again. "And then Ian comes over, an' he's not laughing, but you can tell he thinks it's funny. So my mom gets even madder. Ian says, 'Mary, I think it would be wise if you allowed these boys to lower their sails, lest you lose your sheets. I'll watch them.'"

"So Lauchie's mom doesn't say yes, and she doesn't say no; she just goes back to the house, with the two ladies following her."

"Ian gets all serious looking and says, 'Get those sheets down as fast as you can and mind those slippery branches.' He's standin' there, all stern looking, watching us. He keeps looking away, and I know he's trying not to laugh, but I also know that I'm in deep trouble."

"The wind's still blowing hard," Angus explained, "and Lauchie and I cut the strings and get all the stuff down. But it's no fun anymore. We're wet, the sheets are icy, we're getting' cold."

"We get down and pick up all the stuff," Lauchie said. "Ian tells us to take it to his place, for now."

"Yah, he tells Lauchie that it might be a good idea to behave for a while. He mutters, 'Big storm brewin' in the north'—meaning Lauchie's house. I didn't visit Lauchie for about a week."

Moose sat up, rubbing the grass off his elbow. "So what did your mom do?"

Lauchie grinned. "Ah, well, by the time we got to Ian's, Aunt Grace is already on the phone. You could tell by the conversation that my mom's pretty wrought up." He looked down, the grin fading. "I felt so bad. After a while, they're still on the phone and Aunt Grace is laughing, you know how it is. She's saying stuff like, 'I'll keep them here for a while, dah-da, dah-da, dee-da.' When I got home later, feelin' real stupid and carrying the sheets, all Mom said was, 'Wash those sheets,' but she was all super-calm and flat-eyed. It was awful—felt like I'd betrayed her."

They all sat quietly for a moment. Moose plucked a blade of grass to chew. Angus stared up into the tree. "I thought about that time," he said, "when we read the old letter."

"Yah. Me, too," Lauchie said as he stood up, brushing grass from his jeans. "It's probably suppertime. Let's go."

As Moose stood up, he gave Angus's ankle a shake. "We did crazy stuff like that, too. In the spring we used to get old rotten logs and stuff in the woods and try to dam up the creek. We'd work at it all Saturday, getting wet and muddy, and then bust it at the end of the day. Watch the big flood wave go down stream."

"That's amazing," Lauchie said as they walked toward the house. "Angus and I used to do the same thing every spring."

"Guess it's just natural," Moose said. "One year we got carried away and used a half a cord of my dad's pulpwood. We figured we'd get it back, but when we busted the dam, it went beautiful. That pulp must've gone all the way to Bras d'Or Lake."

"What did your dad do?" Angus asked. "Mine would have killed me."

"After a good cussin' out, I stacked pulp logs for three Saturdays."

Lauchie held the screen door open for Angus and Moose. "It's strange. I think you could take any kids, from anywhere in the world, put them in the same place and they'd do the same dumb stuff."

After supper Mary put the big pail of super chocolate ice cream on the table with some spoons and bowls. "Okay, you can dig for yourselves." She carefully deboned three herring and put them in Dog's dish, adding all the meal scraps, and then she poured the remnants of the teapot in a separate bowl with a little water. "Lauchie, take Dog his supper, please."

Lauchie took a big scoop of ice cream and plopped it on top of Dog's dinner. He took it outside.

Moose looked at Mary. "Does he ever have dog food?"

The screen door closed behind Lauchie.

She shook her head. "Never."

They did the dishes and clean-up for Mary, mostly guilt-tripped by Moose, who was being a good guest. Angus got some more ice cream and they watched television.

At about ten Angus stood and stretched. "I've gottah go home. Lauchie, don't forget, we're doing some exploring tomorrow afternoon. 'Night, Moose. Good to see you. I'll probably see you on the wharf in the morning."

"You bet. 'Night, Angus."

Lauchie stood up, too. "There's a camp cot stashed behind the sofa. Let's get it set up upstairs. It'll be 4:30 A.M. in no time."

They made up the cot in Lauchie's room.

"Give me a kick in the morning," Moose said.

"Okay."

"It'll be nice to be on the boat."

"Yah. See you in the morning."

Fishing with three in the boat made for an easier day. Moose had never fished lobster, but he knew

129

the sea and he knew boats. It was an interesting experience for Lauchie, because he found himself watching and listening more than he would if he'd been with Angus. Ian and Moose chatted comfortably, alike in their easy sociability.

They were pulling traps just off Shag Rock; cormorants were perched on it, drying their wings. Lauchie noted the catch in his project log book, and then pointed with the book at Shag Rock. "Remember in the old letter, when they were looking through the glass at a shaggy rock with cormorants on it?"

"Incredible—could be the same place."

"Hope so."

They'd just hauled three traps and spread them across the small stern deck. Moose opened one that had five lobsters in it; two of them were market size. "Mother sea is most kind," he quipped, giving Lauchie a nudge.

"A good name for her," Ian agreed. "Are we not lucky to be out here fishin' today and callin' it work?"

They all looked at one another and grinned. It wasn't about work being easy; most of the time it wasn't. They grinned with the understanding of their common ties to the sea and the acknowledgment of that special bond.

When they docked, Moose's dad was there with the truck, but he didn't seem in a great rush. Angus was already in. Moose and Lauchie and Angus talked while they sorted the lobsters and Ian went off to talk to Moose's dad. Lauchie looked up from his work and noticed that the two men were watching them while they talked. Lauchie banded the claw of a big market lobster. "What do you think, Moose? They talkin' fish, woods, or hockey?"

"All three, I'd guess. It was nice working with Ian. He's a good man."

"Been good to me. Kinda stood in for my dad, ya know."

The lobsters were finished. They all looked out over the sea. "Thanks for the help today," Lauchie said, turning to Moose.

"Ah, it was a good time. The woods won't be quite as nice. I'm going trout fishin' Sunday. I know some special spots. You guys want to come?"

"Sure," Lauchie said. "Sounds great."

Moose ambled down the wharf, toward his dad. He half-turned, half-waved. "Call you Friday."

Lauchie nodded, "Friday." He turned to Angus and said, "See you after lunch." He watched Moose climb into his dad's truck on the roll, watched their rooster-tail of dust drift over the dried swamp. Ian had backed up his truck to turn around. Lauchie opened the door and climbed into the cab.

Ian let the truck roll forward and said to Lauchie, "A pleasant day's work, that."

"Yes."

11

MAC

Since the second storm of the season had passed Ian and Lauchie had been fishing the deepest traps, then moving them in closer to shore, a few each day.

Overnight a cold front had slipped south over the warm water, causing a dense, chill fog. They would be able to work, finding their way from buoy to buoy, but they wouldn't be able to see anything before sunrise.

Ian turned off the truck and left the running lights on. They got their thermoses and settled in to drink tea and wait it out. Lauchie watched the bouncing rods of light in the dense fog as Dan Angus's truck crept down the wharf lane and pulled up beside them, then another, and another behind him. He could hear the truck doors clunk as fishermen got out to visit while they waited. When Dan Angus came over, Lauchie scrambled out with his tea to go and see Angus; Dan Angus took his place in Ian's truck.

Lauchie shivered and hunched his shoulders.

Everything was wet, even the air. He hurried over to Dan Angus's truck and jumped in on the driver's side. "Going to be a long one," Lauchie said, catching Angus's grin in the flash of the cab light.

"Yah, just 'cause we want to go treasure hunting," Angus said.

It had brightened enough to see the droplets on the windshield. "It'll burn off soon as the sun comes up," Lauchie predicted. He grinned to himself in the darkened cab as he realized that he'd just said what everyone else was probably saying, and he shivered with the awareness that he was a fisherman. If this were last year, he'd be sleeping in bed now—a kid.

"Ian says they decided to blow the big rock that's just off the wharf," Lauchie said.

"Yah. The miners are going to do it for us. It'll be a big show."

"They'll have to wait for low tide to drill the holes for the dynamite," Lauchie said.

Angus scrunched himself up against the truck door, stretching out his legs, getting himself ready to say something. "Grandmother," he said. "Has she got some special powers, ya think?"

Lauchie turned the cab light on, put his thermos cup on the dash, and poured some tea, watching its steam coil dully against the windshield, then turned out the light. "I think she knows special things because she is really in touch with nature; she notices what we don't. Like when she senses things,

133

she doesn't wonder, Could it be this, could it be that. She *knows*. I think that's a power."

"Yah, but is it like a religion?" Angus asked.

"Maybe for Grandmother. I don't know." Lauchie paused, holding the thought. "I think it's like this: Grandmother doesn't tell anyone to believe or not believe anything. I think she'd say that the earth, sea, air, plants, and animals are good. We should respect them, not abuse them."

Angus sighed, scrunching into another awkward thinking position. "Well, who could argue with that? I just think that she's a special wise person."

"Like a lot of times, doin' good things seems kind of wimpoid. She takes the wimpy out of doin' good things."

"Exactly!" Angus laughed. "I was just wondering if this was like spooky hokum stuff or something."

"Yah, I know. But what's spooky about someone who says, 'What is, is'?"

They stared at the fog slowly lightening like a great emptiness beyond them. Drops on the windshield that grew too heavy to resist the pull of gravity suddenly streaked downward in jagged paths. "I think someone that close to nature can know things, or do things, that are hard to explain," Lauchie said. "I don't think that's spooky."

"Want to know what I think?" Angus asked, tapping the windshield to release a heavy droplet. "I think the big difference between Grandmother and other people is that she sees that all the things in nature are as special as she is, and that makes *her* special."

"Yah," Lauchie agreed. "I bet that's why she's so happy and interesting. She loves the world she lives in."

Their early-morning philosophy was interrupted by the sound of Ian getting out of the truck beside them and rapping on their roof. "Time to gear up and get out there." As though everyone else had the same thought, men began spilling out of all the trucks.

Lauchie winched a box of bait down to the boat. Below him Ian appeared to hover above the dim outline of the gunnels, his legs hidden in the dark fog. Objects bumping the boats echoed tinnily in the thick air, and men on the wharf seemed to suddenly float into Lauchie's small circle of vision, then drift back out. The first motor started with a hoarse growl in the heavy silence, then another, and soon they were all under way, each boat moving slowly, keeping tight to the wharf to avoid the big rock cloaked in fog, and then fanning quickly out of sight, watching and listening for one another.

Ian and Lauchie traveled out slowly in a thirty- or forty-foot circle of vision that seemed to travel with them. The air had a damp texture that left chill droplets on every surface. The sea was flat, gray, and oily-looking, as though the fog held it down. Soon they found their first buoy, then another and another. They fished the inside first because they couldn't move traps until the fog lifted.

Lauchie heard a great lazy splash, resonant in the

dense air, like a sound in slow motion. His first thought was breaking water. Had they drifted in somehow? Then he realized that he was holding a buoy that he knew was well out.

"Black fish," Ian said with a grin. "There must be mackerel about. We'll have mackerel in the bait net, for sure."

The next disturbance was only thirty feet from the boat, a large pilot whale, about nineteen feet long. It breached in a graceful slow arc through the calm surface, glistening black in the dim fog, highlighted by the foam of disturbed water all about it. Lauchie stared at it, eye to eye. He saw not the flat eye of a fish but a knowing, intelligent eye, seeming to be as curious of Lauchie as he was of it. The whale continued its arc back into the water in a soft, languid splash, then its tail rose with a powerful, easy flick, and it was gone, the boat rocking in its wake. Another repeated the same pattern, almost out of range of Lauchie's vision. He was shaking with the excitement of it and wanted, in his heart, to pursue them, just to watch them. Ian anticipated his thoughts, sounding gruff over the sound of the motor.

"We'll leave them be. They'll be about for the day, most likely."

By eight the fog had lifted, burned off by the sun and helped by a light breeze. The whales could still be seen, a pod of about forty, broken into small groups, but they were moving slowly west along the coast, about a half-mile beyond Shag Rock.

The bait net was heavy with mackerel . . . and with something else. It was a young salmon, just small enough to be caught in the bait-net mesh. It was about seven and half pounds and had caught at the swing end of the net. The rest of the school had fortunately passed unhindered. The first look on Ian's face was one of pure love as he murmured, "Now, what have we here?" Then he got his lecturing look in place and kept it there while they cleared the net, then tied up. The salmon was dead in the net. Ian placed it carefully under his oiler top, beneath the shade of the bow deck. Then he and Lauchie washed their hands in the sea and sat on a couple of crates for tea.

Lauchie noted Ian's serious, thoughtful, look—a definite sermonizing look, he thought—and said nothing as he watched Ian pour his tea.

"I want you to understand, boy, this is a decision you'll have to make some day. The law says I've got to throw that salmon to the sea gulls; there are no licenses for it. It's a proper law for a good reason, and if that fish were alive, I'd release it." He looked off at the island for a moment, then looked back. "I could lose my license for having that fish aboard." He looked back at the island, as though it held an answer. "We've fished this shore for generations, and there's another law. I'll not waste that fine fish to the gulls. I just want you to be clear in your mind that I'm breakin' a law and you've no part in it. It's a matter of conscience," he said bearishly. "And common sense," he added in a lighter tone.

Lauchie nodded, thinking, What a day this has been. He totally agreed with Ian and was not in any way surprised. It was different and exciting because he was part of it. Kids did things that they weren't supposed to, but this was an adult delinquency and he was in on it. It also confirmed what he'd begun to suspect. Growing up didn't change who you were, nor were the hard decisions of the schoolyard much different from those of the working world.

Just before they got back to the wharf, Ian pulled up the leg of his oilers and dumped the salmon head-down in his rubber boot, pulling his oilers back down over the boot. When they docked, there was a cheerful-looking man with light sandy hair talking to Angus, which caused a momentary look of consternation on Ian's face. The stranger was no fisherman; he wore hard shoes and a casual shirt and jeans, but his clothes didn't have a working look. Lauchie busied himself with unloading the catch, trying to imagine who it might be. When he climbed up the ladder, Angus introduced him.

"Lauchie, this is Dr. Macdonald from Halifax Museum. He came to see the letter."

As they shook hands, Lauchie noticed a look of relief on Ian's face as he said, "I'll look after this. You see to your guest." He picked out eight nice canners. "Here, take these to your mother." Dr. Macdonald raised one eyebrow in an appreciative, comical way.

As they were leaving, Dan Angus was coming down the wharf. "Did you get mackerel in your net?"

Lauchie heard Ian murmur, "Yes and more. I'll be changin' my socks before supper."

Dan Angus grinned. "Well, a man of such refinement would be entertaining, I suppose?"

"And some cards after."

Ian and Dan Angus were still laughing as Lauchie, Angus, and the doctor walked down the wharf, and Lauchie had the feeling that Dr. Macdonald was tuned to the conversation behind them.

"I stopped at the house and met your mother," he was saying as they approached his Volkswagen. "We talked a bit, and she sent me down to meet you boys."

Angus pushed the passenger seat forward and climbed into the back of the little car. Lauchie got into the front.

"Are you interested in treasure, Dr. Macdonald?" Lauchie asked as they drove up the wharf lane.

"Well, a letter almost four hundred years old is a treasure. What it says is a different matter," he said, then added, "I was discreet at the wharf. And please call me Mac."

"Have you seen what it says?" Lauchie asked, feeling a bit pushy and determined to check this guy out before trusting him.

"No, your mother said I had to deal with you. I must admit I'm very interested."

"We'd like to know what you think of it, but it has to stay secret."

Mac reached over to shake hands with the boys,

laughing as his car skittered on the loose gravel. "Agreed," he said.

When they reached Lauchie's house, Mac hollered at the kitchen door, much as Ian would have, "Hello, Mary, I'm back again." Dog watched him with a look of relaxed interest, a point in Mac's favor that Lauchie noted.

"Hello again, Mac. Did an old curmudgeon, by any chance, send some lobsters for lunch?"

"The gentleman surely did. I was tempted to buy some, but I know the fishermen like to sell to the buyers."

"How'd you know that?" Angus asked.

"Well, I wasn't born in a museum, you know. My dad still runs a dragger out of Lunenburg, and I did my time on her."

Angus and Lauchie exchanged quick glances. This guy was maybe okay.

Lauchie ran up the stairs to his room to get the tissue-wrapped bundle and their notes. When he returned, Mac was laying out sheets of unbleached paper, a special-looking, shallow box, and a large magnifying glass.

Lauchie handed him the bundle, and Mac folded back the tissues. *"Yes,"* he breathed. "Such condition! He must have heated the container to make it seal like that. It survived all those years."

The big lobster pot was beginning to boil. "Will the kitchen steam do any harm?" Mary asked.

"A bit would almost be good," Mac mumbled,

engrossed in his study. Then suddenly becoming aware, he added, "I'm being rude. Your lunch will be ready. Angus, help me move this to the living room. If you will take the box. . . ." They quickly moved the original to a safe table in the living room and returned to the kitchen.

"Sit, Mac," Mary demanded as Lauchie handed Mac their notes.

"Thank you, Lauchie," Mac said, as he pulled up a chair to the kitchen table.

"Was it hard to find us here?" Angus asked.

"No, I've got a cabin just up by Red River," Mac answered, "so I know the area well."

"Then you know lobsters," Mary said, putting them on the table. "Lauchie, get the potatoes and greens, please."

They began to eat, making conversation, but Mac's eyes kept straying to the notes. "You worked a dragger," Lauchie said.

"Yes, when I was your age, and all through university. My grandfather worked a salt banker," he added with a grin.

Mary looked up quickly at Mac and said, "Mac, you're being polite. Eat your lobster and I'll read." Everyone laughed. She scooped up the notes and began to read.

It was obvious to Lauchie and Angus that they weren't going to start their search that day, but Mac was very amusing, and sprinkled through his conversation about the old letter were stories of other documents and how he had found them. He made the idea of research and museum work sound interesting, even exciting. He studied the papers carefully and tried to convince them that they should be in the museum, where they would be protected, and others could see them. The problem was that it would make them public information. "What if we agreed to make the source of the information a secret?" Mac suggested.

"No good," Lauchie said. "The story puts them on this side of the island, and Sea Dog is not much of a stretch for Sea Wolf."

"I think you're right," Mac agreed. "Would some time limit . . . No, no guarantee there."

"I think it would be okay for you to hold them secretly," Lauchie said, looking at Angus and catching a nod of agreement. "That way you can protect them and study them while we go treasure hunting."

"Excellent solution," Mac agreed. "I'll give you a receipt for them."

They got Mac telling stories that his granddad had told about the salt banker days when the *Blue Nose* was just one of many fine schooners, and about adventures he'd had aboard his dad's dragger.

"Now," he said, "may I take you all out to supper tonight to celebrate our bargain?"

"That would be wonderful," Mary said.

Lauchie didn't consult Angus. "Not us. But

thanks. We'd just talk about treasure, and besides, we've got to get up at four-thirty."

"You kids should come. You have to eat."

"Mom, I can feed myself. Go have a good time."

"You'll just sneak over to Ian's, I bet."

"Well, he'll be curious about the letter and all."

"Lauchie, you sure?"

Mac spoke up, surprising everyone. "Well, he'll eat well, I think. The gentleman who sent the lobsters seemed to have a terrible salmon limp at the wharf."

Mary sputtered, "Lauchie, no" then looked at Mac. "Do they sometimes suffer from salmon limps in Lunenburg, too?"

"Occasional attacks, yes."

Lauchie squared his shoulders. "It was dead in the net and won't be wasted." He glanced at Mac, who gave him the nod.

"I wonder what else that old rogue is teaching you," Mary said, but her eyes danced with devilment, and Mac's reaction had not gone unnoticed.

Mac pushed his chair back, looking about the room. "Mary, thank you for the wonderful lunch, and Lauchie, Angus, it's been a pleasure talking to you. I'm so glad that you let me see this bit of lost history. I'd like to take the letter with me now, and study it this afternoon, if I may."

"Yes," Lauchie said. "It's been nice meeting you. Let us know what you find out, but please remember that no one else can see it."

Angus nodded. "Nice meetin' you."

Mac got up and headed for the door. "I'll let you know anything that I discover." He paused to shake hands with Lauchie and Angus. "Mary, could I pick you up at six-thirty for supper? Is that a good time?"

"Perfect."

"I'll see you then." Lauchie opened the door for Mac.

Mac nodded. "Good luck with your treasure hunting."

Lauchie kept the door open. "Come on, Angus. Let's go plan tomorrow."

"Lauchie," Mary said, "the lawn comes before the treasure, okay?"

"Sure, sure—after supper, when it's cooler."

Lauchie and Angus went to Ian and Aunt Grace's for supper, along with Dan Angus and Marge. They talked about Mac and agreed that he seemed like an okay guy, for a mainlander. Ian roared with laughter when he heard about the salmon limp, especially since he was eating salmon at that moment.

After supper Lauchie borrowed Ian's rider mower. He and Angus forgot what a chore it was supposed to be and did a great job. They started the mower at Ian's and cut the path between their houses and around the apple tree. Angus even weed-whacked around the mailbox.

It was getting dark by the time they finished, and they took Cokes out on the newly cut lawn, under the apple tree. The cut grass smelled good, and the sea was still luminous and calm, darkly reflecting the island.

"What a big day," Angus said. "You owe me one for the lawn, Lauchie. I want points with your mom for this."

"Yah, she'll love it. Most people just cut the lawn. She's got this hairdresser's thing. She wants me to style it."

"I gottah go before I fall asleep. See you at the wharf."

Dog reappeared; he had taken off while the lawn mower was running. He greeted Angus with a nudge to his leg, and then lay down beside Lauchie. They watched Angus ride slowly home, weaving in big lazy arcs down the darkening road, oblivious to the halo of gnats around his head.

Gazing out at the darkening sea, Lauchie thought about Mac working on a dragger. It occurred to him that he hadn't had the dream of his father's death in a long time, and the thought was tinged with guilt. "I'm a weird kid," he muttered to Dog. "It wasn't what you'd call a fun dream. Feels like things are changing every day."

Dog rested his head in Lauchie's lap, and rolled his eyes up to watch him. Lauchie leaned back against the trunk of the big apple tree. The grass began to dampen, and the still air seemed filled with the white noise of a million tiny things settling and contracting as the air cooled and the dew formed. He gave Dog's ears a last ruffle, picked up the Coke bottles, brushed the grass cuttings from his jeans, and went into the house.

12

RESEARCH

The next day all the talk was about the big rock just shoreward of the wharf. Three holes had already been bored deep into the rock and plugged. In the late afternoon everyone planned to take his boat out to the safety of the sea. The rock would be packed with explosives and blown.

"If we're careful," Angus said, "we can still do our search. We'll have a perfect view from up there."

"Yah, and it's too high for anyone else to bother climbing. We'll grab a quick lunch and get on up there before anybody arrives at the wharf."

At lunchtime, Mary gave Lauchie a message from Mac. She had written down the specific part. He had been doing tests on the original letter and had noticed a discrepancy between what he read and what he remembered of their translation. The blurred line that they had taken to say "beneath a small cairn I sank a hole just south of a large square rock" actually said "beneath a small caved-in sinkhole just south of a large square rock." This was interesting but no help. In fact, it was bad news.

Throughout the area there were places where gypsum, a soft, chalky stone, had dissolved and crumbled away. The ground would cave in, leaving a crater from a few feet across to a lake-sized hole. The problem was that there were no sinkholes up on that hill.

Now they were standing in Angus's driveway with their bikes. Lauchie had a coil of half-inch rope draped bandolier-style across his chest. He had two pieces of half-inch steel rebar, each about a foot and a half long. He held them by clamping them across the handlebars of his bike. Angus had another coil of rope and two more steel rods. The other tools were still on top of the hill.

"If it's a sinkhole," Angus said, "We're sunk, 'cause it's sunk somewhere out in the sea."

"Well, let's go anyway. We'll take the stuff up there and think it through."

"Yah," Angus said. "We'll give it one more try. It's not the treasure that bothers me; it's not knowing what happened and losing the search."

They rode down to the wharf. The bad news seemed to wipe out their energy, and the hill that had held such promise and excitement now seemed steep and unrelenting in the hot afternoon.

When they reached the top, they wandered around picking berries, feeling at a loss with no clear plan.

"Hey," Angus said, "this isn't the worst place to spend an afternoon."

They sat, this time on the crow's nest side, over the cliff. It occurred to Lauchie that he had sat in this same spot the morning of his "meditation." Dog settled on the cliff edge with his paws hanging over and his nose to the wind.

The crow's nest was about two feet across and made of small sticks and hay, rougher looking than the nests of other birds. The glitter of bits of foil and glass confirmed the crows' love of shiny things. The season's young crows had already learned to fly, so the nest was deserted.

Lauchie reached behind his back, found some pebbles, and began tossing them into the nest. They weren't hanging out far enough to see the whole nest because the top of the cliff canted out at the top, but it was still too easy to hit the nest.

"Okay," Angus said. "You can't just pitch them in. You have to lob them up at least ten feet and bomb the nest."

"First guy to get ten wins." The treasure was momentarily forgotten, and they were just old friends whiling away a summer afternoon and arguing the points of a game that they'd made up.

"If we can't come up with treasure, at least we'll still see them blow the big rock," Angus remarked.

"It'll make the harbor safer, comin' in."

"Sure, if they don't blow up the wharf while they're at it."

One of Angus's stones kicked off the outer edge of the nest and bounced nicely inward, toward the cliff. "That's nine for me," he said.

"No way," Lauchie argued. "I heard it bounce down the cliff."

"Bull! It didn't splash. It's in."

"You can't hear it splash, anyway."

They argued back and forth for a while, not really caring much, and then it happened again with a larger stone. They both heard its rattling descent but saw no bouncing rock on the cliff side. It was strange. They abandoned the game and began firing bigger rocks straight down toward the rear of the nest. The third shot scored, and they listened to it careening unseen. Lauchie searched until he found a larger, irregularly shaped rock that he tied to the end of the rope.

They maneuvered the rope so that it swung out and then in toward the nest. After several tries, one swing went a little high, cleared the nest, and seemed to keep swinging into the cliffside. It stopped, leaving the rope slack. Angus snapped the rope, sending a wave rippling down its length, and the rock must have moved, because it took up the slack. Angus got down on his belly, reached out, and sent another ripple down the rope, and then another. It took more of the slack. He looked up and locked eyes with Lauchie, who was kneeling beside him. "In a small caved-in sinkhole behind a big square rock," Angus said.

Lauchie bumped his fist on Angus's shoulder. "This is it. Yes!"

They both stared down at the boulders at the foot of the cliff. They were water-worn, some almost lozenge-shaped, while others had been cracked apart by ice and frost. Any one of them might once have been the large square rock. "So where do we go from here?" Angus asked.

"Not where, but how. We've got to think this one out carefully," Lauchie said.

"You think anyone will come around here when the boats go out for the blast?"

"Nah. They'll all stay together and go west, so they can watch it."

They decided to drive in the iron stakes to give themselves time to think about possible problems, aside from the sheer terror of hanging over the edge of a cliff on a rope. They kept hitting rock and had to try several places before they got good purchase. Finally, both bars were deeply embedded and angled back away from the cliff edge. They decided that one of them would go down and the other would stay as backup until they were sure that they could trust the anchorage. They tied rope on each of the pitons, one for a climbing rope and one as a safety. Lauchie would go first because he was lighter, and Angus would guide and hold the back-up rope.

They solemnly shook hands, then started laughing nervously. Lauchie threw the climbing rope over the edge. The loose pebbles that it sent cascading to the sea below didn't make him feel any better. He tied the back-up rope around his waist and handed the slack to Angus so that he could guide it and keep it out of the way. He got down on his belly and began squirming backward over the lip, fearing that if he thought about it anymore he'd surely lose his courage.

Lauchie held the rope tightly in a two-handed grip, and as his feet swung out over the cliff, he trapped the rope by clamping his right foot over his left. He had the rope wrapped from his right side around behind him and then from the left side it came back to the front, so that the friction would help him. They had both climbed ropes often enough, but never suspended a hundred or so feet above a tumble of boulders.

As Lauchie began to ease over the cliff edge, Dog jumped up and braced his feet in front of Lauchie, trying to grab a mouthful of his T-shirt. "Get away, Dog," he hollered, laughing at Dog's concern. The laughter must have reassured Dog, because he backed off with a plaintive whine and stood beside Angus, watching intently.

Lauchie gave a last squirm and he was over the edge in a disconcerting rain of shale and scree. He glanced up at Angus, who looked as frightened as he felt, and he could see Angus's hands already white with the intensity of his grip on the safety rope. Beside him stood Dog, combining gruff, throaty grumbles with anxious whines. A last nod, and Lauchie was on his way down, looking now straight into the face of the cliff.

The first few feet were the most terrifying because the lip held him free of the cliff face, and every movement seemed to bring another hail of debris down on top of him. Now that he was committed, he lowered himself quickly, eager to get it over with, and soon he was hanging above the nest. He gingerly kicked the nest off the ledge. Keeping a good grip on the rope, he tested the ledge. If it was going to break away, he wanted it to happen while he was still on the rope. He heard Angus holler from above, "You okay?"

"Yah. Just testing the ledge. It feels solid."

Lauchie still held tight to the rope as he gingerly let his weight settle on the ledge. Seeing it up close, he had more faith in it. It was large, not so much because it protruded, but because it cut back into the cliff face.

Angus could not see him. He had to stand back from the edge to hold the rope and watch the pegs. "You can let out some slack now. I'm there," Lauchie shouted.

He was facing cliffside and he slowly lowered himself to a squatting position, still holding the rope for balance. It was only then that he started to tremble, partly from the extended strain on his hands and arms but more from plain old fear and the overcharge of adrenaline racing through his system.

He took in the new view, which was not possible from above, or from the sea. A large upward-pointing triangle had broken out of the cliff face. It formed the ledge and shaped an opening into the cliff. It was about four feet high and about three feet wide and sloped steeply down so that from the sea it would appear to be just a shadowed crevice in the rock. From above it was protected from view by the overhang, and also by a bulge in the cliff face. The ceiling of the cave sloped less sharply than the floor, so that the ceiling height increased as the cave went deeper. The sun had swung west of the opening and dim, indirect light lit the cave entrance, allowing Lauchie to see only a short distance into the interior.

He was feeling a bit more confident now, simply because he'd been on the ledge for a while. He suddenly realized that Angus was shouting. "So what do you see? What's there?" Lauchie stood up, holding the rope for support, and brashly leaned out to describe it all, beginning to feel braver. He couldn't help but laugh at the sight of Angus's concerned expression over the rim of the cliff, and Dog's equally worried look beside him. Lauchie also realized that what Angus saw was a kid perched on a ledge high above the sea, while what he saw was Angus only a few feet away on familiar solid ground. He decided not to look down.

"It's a cave, and big, I think. It's too dark to see very far in. We'll need lights and stuff."

They decided that Lauchie should come back up, because once they both went down there would be no one for backup. Lauchie's trip up would be one more test of their equipment, with Angus still there to guide the safety line and watch the pitons.

"Okay," Lauchie said. "Let's do it." Angus disappeared, going back to his position by the pegs. Lauchie began his climb.

Most frightening was that first commitment to swing clear of the ledge, dangling free, dependent on the rope. It was like that instant before you dive off a high board followed by the realization that you can no longer change your mind. The positive action of climbing was a bit better than the descent except that the process was reversed.

Instead of getting closer and closer to the cliff face, he was now hanging farther and farther out. The dreaded moment was the changeover from rope climbing to the combined climb and scramble over the lip. Lauchie broke into a terrified sweat. Why did I do this? he wondered. If anything were to shake loose or go wrong, it would happen now. Only the awareness that he was seconds from safety gave him the courage to reach up over the lip. First he was feeling the rough scrabble of the cliff face, then the reassuring texture of sun-warmed grass, then Angus's hand about his wrist. He was up and over.

Lauchie lay for a moment on his back, catching his breath, feeling the warm familiar grass on his back, and enduring a face licking from Dog. He sat up slowly and looked about at the normal sights. Everything seemed more vivid and intense, as though his seeing were magnified. He looked at Angus and grinned. "It's gottah be there." He described everything he'd seen, and they began to make plans for what they would need.

"I'll get my backpack," Lauchie said. "We'll need

a couple of sweaters and candles and matches in case something happens to our lights."

"We need flashlights and extra batteries. Some string to hang the lights from around our necks," Angus said.

"Okay," Lauchie said. "Let's get another short length of rope and a peg to hang the stuff on while we climb down."

"How about a two-by-four to go across the cave mouth to tie off on?"

"Yah, perfect." Lauchie said. "And I'm going to bring my compass."

"Let's do it now," Angus suggested. "If we wait, I'll either go crazy or chicken out."

"Me, too," Lauchie agreed.

They went down the hill in a much better mood than they had come up in, the excitement of blowing the big rock shoved from their minds. Even if there were no treasure, there was a cave that no one else knew about.

"Lauchie, this is our total absolute secret."

"Yah. Crow Cave."

13

SPELUNKERS

Sometime in the ancient past the sinkhole had formed. Then, acting like a little reservoir, it had trapped water. As years went by, the water found drainage through tiny cracks between the soft gypsum and the harder limestone.

Over time, a shaft formed, and layers of strata gave way, creating a wedgelike cavern with a wide base at the bottom, which slowly worked its way upward, eventually caving in at the surface.

In the early 1600s the cave was probably just a small depression at the surface, giving no indication of the huge, hidden chamber below. Over the years the sea cliff wore its way closer to the sinkhole. Then some long-ago spring the north side of the sinkhole fell into the sea, and the trauma of that disruption opened the last few feet to the cave below.

Lauchie and Angus arrived at the top of the cliff with everything they needed. They had made Dog stay home. The first thing they did was dig away part of the overhanging lip of the cliff so that it formed more of a ramp than of a drop into space. To any passerby it would appear to be a natural occurrence, and the bulge of the cliff face would still protect their secret.

They drove in another steel bar, and on the short rope they hung their backpack, the two-by-four, their gear, and the extra rope. It was all out of the way but within easy reach from the mouth of the cave.

Lauchie elected to go first, tying the backup safety rope once more around his waist. He quickly wiggled over the edge, finding it much easier with some of the lip cut away, but he still broke out in a cold sweat. He tried to block out the sound of the surf pounding at the base of the cliff and concentrated on his inch-by-inch progress down the rope.

Lauchie heard a rattling from above and looked up to see a stone-encrusted clod of overhung sod that they had missed sliding over the lip. He gripped the rope and tucked his head in.

Instantly, it hit with a painful thump on his left shoulder. He clung to the rope, shaking and waiting for the pain to pass, then continued the short distance to the safety of the ledge. He caught his breath while untying the safety rope, then tried to sound casual as he called up to Angus. "Okay, you can pull up the safety rope now. I'll hold the other one tight for you." Lauchie massaged his shoulder; it would be bruised, but the pain was beginning to recede.

Angus didn't say anything, but soon Lauchie could see his sneakers edging over the crest. He called encouragement, glad that it was Angus on the rope and not himself.

"Swing in. I'll grab you."

They were both on the ledge.

"That was some hairy," Angus exclaimed with a grin of pride.

They took turns facing the cliff and slowly edging down to a sitting position on the ledge. Next they grabbed the rope with their gear on it and carefully slipped the two-by-four underneath them, then squirmed about as they worked one end of the long rope under the two-by-four so that they could tie it off.

They looked at each other, both grinning so hard it hurt. "Right now," Angus said, "this minute, is the most exciting minute of my life."

"You tellin' me that coming down the rope was boring?"

"You know what I mean."

Lauchie nodded. "Yah. We've found a secret cave."

They got out their flashlights and shone them down into the cave. Angus threw the rope in as far as he could and it shone bright and yellow on the smooth, gray, steep floor. About forty feet beyond it, the cave seemed to end in a craggy cliff-like wall that hadn't been visible without the lights.

Angus carefully stood up, tested the rope, and went in backwards. "Let's do it."

The rope was little more than a precaution, and in moments they were down to the wall.

Up close the wall was harder to see because their flashlights revealed only small circles of it at once. They soon discovered that it was better to climb back up the slope and shine the lights down from a greater distance. The wall was different from the rest of the cave, but it took a while to realize why.

"It's the strata," Lauchie said. "It's going the wrong way."

"You're right. It goes straight up and down, and the cave strata slopes down on an angle."

"It's part of the roof. I think the inside broke first, and it swung down instead of just dropping."

"So there's more cave," Angus said, "and it looks blocked."

"It can't be blocked everywhere," Lauchie reasoned.

It was. The big slab that had fallen was wedged into the cave entrance like an oversized stopper. Any projections that may have made an entrance along the sides had broken off, either when it fell or sometime later from the pressure and weight. They swung their lights back and forth over the surface, looking for a way in, and saw nothing but rock face that wasn't even vertical but slanted back toward them. They also noticed that the big slab still had an unworn look. It wasn't smooth like the sides. A few broken chunks lay covered in dust at the foot of the obstruction.

"It looks new," Lauchie said.

"Well, there's nothing in here to wear it down."

Lauchie had an idea. He shone his light across the smooth-looking floor, which was so deep in dust that it had a uniform look, like snow-covered ground. Their footprints showed up darkly shadowed in the low light beam. Down the center, almost where they had come down the rope, there was the long shadow of a depression, like a shallow ditch. "Look at that," Lauchie said, aiming his light along the trench and following it to the wall, where a medium-sized rock had fallen. "It's like a ditch."

They half-ran and half-slid to the spot and rolled the rock out of the way. The ditch ran under the obstruction. They scraped back the debris and saw a shallow, dust-free trench continuing under the big barrier. "I think we can make it through," Lauchie said. "I'll try first, 'cause I'm smaller."

"No way," Angus argued. "If you get stuck, I can't go in for you without getting stuck. If I get stuck, maybe you can get me out. Besides, if I get through, then we know that you can get in and get out again. So I go in first."

"Angus, you've got a real twisted mind. Logical, but twisted." Lauchie went back up the rope to get the backpack with the candles and matches and sweaters and extra batteries, while Angus tied the other end of the rope around his left ankle. When Lauchie returned, they sat on the overturned rock and had a conference. They decided to take their belts off, thinking that it would be better to lose their pants than get snagged by a belt that couldn't be reached. They put their flashlight strings around their necks, intending to keep them out in front of them at all times, and they each tied a jackknife on the string where they could get at it. Candles and matches went in their hip pockets so that they wouldn't get broken.

"Okay," Angus said. "Let's do it."

"Don't go forward until you're sure that there's something under you," Lauchie cautioned as Angus began to wiggle under the rock.

Lauchie watched Angus's sneakers disappear, watched the rope inch into the tunnel. Every second seemed a minute.

"What do you see?"

"Rock." Angus's voice came back muffled and distorted.

"Now what do you see?"

"More rock."

The rope jerked forward, stopped, then took a quick couple of feet, then a fast four feet. Lauchie hollered, "Angus!"

There was a moment's pause and then a distorted laugh. "Hey, come on in. It's a piece of cake."

Lauchie tied the backpack to the rope, making it into a streamlined bundle. "Okay, pull the backpack through." He guided the rope through his hands to avoid loops.

"It's clear."

Lauchie squirmed in, following Angus's rope and pushing his light in front of him. It was almost impossible to see anything because the light shone right in front of his nose, making a big splash of bright light, until he learned to shield it. The position that he was in was the same position he so vividly imagined when he heard all the late-night stories about the old bootleg coal mines. Stories about men following small seams of coal in cramped, wet tunnels, depending on each other for their very lives. They were buddies, but in the mines "buddy" had a very special meaning. It was a pact to look out for one another, no matter what. Suddenly, a strange echoing voice intruded on his thoughts. *"Rats,"* it murmured.

Lauchie jumped, as much as one can jump in a cramped tunnel, and hit his head. "I'll get you good for that, Angus!" Then he was through, his light shining into Angus's grinning face.

"Hang on to the rope," Angus warned him. "We're on a bit of a ledge, and then it drops." His voice echoed even more than it had on the other side. They were truly underground now, and the word went through Lauchie's mind with all the mystery and implication that it had always carried.

There was a small coal mine just up the road from his house, probably the last family-owned mine on the island. Ian had once arranged to take him down into the miles of tunnel. From that time on Lauchie had understood some of the special mystery of the word "underground" and the phrase "He works below."

Lauchie dug out his candle. "I don't think the air's stale, and there shouldn't be any methane here." He lit the candle, and it burned with a bright, still flame.

"Good air so far," Angus agreed.

They shone their lights around them, finding it as difficult as before to see the whole area because they couldn't see it all at once and had to piece together the segments that the lights revealed. The ledge they were on ran out about ten feet in front of them on the same slope as the cave behind. They edged along the ropes and shone their lights down. There was a drop of about fifteen feet. The little cliff face had broken at right angles to the strata, so that it angled back and in as it dropped. It would be an easy climb down and back on the rope.

Angus pulled the rope tight, testing it, and started down while Lauchie gave him light, then followed in the same way. At the bottom they measured off their remaining rope. It was about thirteen fathoms, which was just under eighty feet.

They scanned the area again with their lights, talking in low voices because the echo was so strong and the darkness so spooky. Lauchie had been aware of a sort of white noise, as when you put a seashell to your ear, but he had ignored it, thinking that it was an effect of the cave. Now it seemed stronger. "Do you hear a faint noise?" he asked Angus.

"Yah. I thought it was just the cave. Maybe there's water somewhere."

Lauchie was swinging his light along in front of him. The cave still widened as it sank, but just in front of them, about thirty feet down the slope, another wall of rock blocked off most of the passage from right to left, which they thought of as north to south. The floor now seemed to tilt to the left as well as downward in front of them. As Lauchie ran his light along the base of the new obstruction, he saw a shape at the end that didn't have the familiar rock-look of the cave. Angus was also staring at the same spot and added his light to it. "Let's check that out. Looks like old wood," he said. They grabbed the rope and backed down the slope, bumping into each other as the wall stopped them sooner than they anticipated.

"This is it! it! it!" Angus hollered, his voice echoing through the cave. "I knew it! It's here."

"It's the treasure chest—been here forever!" Lauchie said pounding Angus's shoulder, his light arcing across the ceiling.

"Hey, be cool," Angus said. "Wait a minute—where's the stuff?" Their lights were shining on the bottom of an old chest or box. The sides and lid were no longer there, and the remnants of steel straps were paper-thin strips of rust that lay on the floor like stains. The wood was so rotted that it crumbled when Angus tried to lift it.

There was no treasure.

"Where is it?" Lauchie wondered out loud as he swung the light about.

On the floor of the cave they could see the

smooth track of the ditch that they had used to get in farther up. "It must have slid down here before the big rock fell," Angus said. "Look—you can still see where the water used to run."

"I think it hit this wall, and the rest of it kept going," Lauchie said, swinging his light around the corner. The light picked up a few more feet of slope, then another wall some distance away.

They followed the slope, hanging on to the last few feet of their rope and looked down . . . to the stream below.

The water sound was not very strong, and the resonant quality of the cave had masked it, blending the sounds into a uniform hum. The drop here was less severe. Off to the left a big slab that had once been somewhere up the slope had slid down to rest at an angle easy for them to climb down. The upper half of the slab still had the sharp, angled, unweathered look of the rocks above, but the lower half was worn and eroded like the boulders on the seashore. They each took turns holding a light while the other climbed down.

The stream was in a rounded chamber with smooth, water-washed sides. There was an oblong pool in the center that was about two feet deep, and the seaward end was dammed by a bar of harder rock that had not worn away. The pool spilled over the dam into another pool. The clear water revealed a bottom of worn rock. The pool looked amber in their lights, and the bouncing light reflected on the wall across from it, painting everything in monotones of dull gold.

They shone their lights back along the way they'd come, looking for the glint of gold. "It isn't here," Lauchie said.

"It's all clean rock: there's no place to hide."

"Gottah be in the water."

They quickly yanked off their socks and shoes and left them on the small apron, rolled up their jeans, scrambled down, and waded in.

"Yow!" Lauchie yelped.

"It's cold," Angus said as they both got out quickly and put their socks back on and then their sweaters, leaving their sneakers.

"This should help," Lauchie said, "sort of like fishing gloves," and he waded back in with a wincing shiver.

They waded over to the little dam and stepped over into the next pool. It was only about a foot lower and held a pleasant surprise. "Water's a bit warmer," Angus exclaimed, scooping some up in his hand to taste. "Salt. It's mixing with seawater."

Lauchie shone his light on the wall and opened the knife that was on his flashlight string. He stooped down and scratched a "V" so that the point came down at the water line. There wasn't much to see in the pool. The ceiling sloped down until it met the water about twenty feet down the length of the pool. At the far end, under the slope, they could see some pale sand on the bottom. Angus cupped his ear to the wall, and Lauchie did the same. They could hear the faint pounding of the sea.

"So we're at sea level," Lauchie pointed out. He crouched down and waded toward the sand, raking his fingers along it. "There's no depth. It's just a skiff of sand on the rock. Let's go the other way."

They stopped under the drop-off, passing their lights all about. "The rest of the chest, and whatever was in it, had to come down here," Lauchie said.

"Yah, but I don't see anything," Angus complained. "I don't see it in the water, and the rock is all smooth here."

"Maybe it got washed away, or just worn away by the water," Lauchie said. "Let's explore upstream while we think about it." He checked his compass. "Warm water's north. Stream's comin' from the south."

They skirted the main pool, avoiding the cold water as long as possible, and entered the south tunnel where it tumbled into the pool. The tunnel was about four feet wide and almost high enough to stand upright in. The sides were smooth because the underground stream had cut the tunnel over the years by wearing the rock lower. There was a very strong flow of water across the four feet. It was about eight inches deep. They walked side by side, shining their lights down on the bottom and following the curves of the stream as it wound its way through the soft rock.

"We can't go uphill like this for long," Angus noted, "or we'll come out in the swamp."

"Lagoon," Lauchie corrected with a laugh. "This must have fed the lagoon at some time in the past. I bet that's what happened to the other creek."

"Right. It must have found a way into this system, instead of feeding the pond. But the underground stream must have always been here."

"I think so, too," Lauchie said. "It seems older than the entrance cave. Maybe when the surface creek broke into this system, it caused the cave to fall in."

They followed another small bend in the stream and came to an enlarged chamber that dead-ended the tunnel. The ceiling rose to about twelve feet high, and the chamber was about ten feet in diameter. There was no floor to the chamber, because its sides fell straight to the water.

They shone their lights down into the water. They could see the sides for a long way down, looking amber in the yellow beams of light. They could see no bottom, and the center of the pool bubbled with effervescence.

"Wow," Angus remarked. "It's coming up under pressure. It must run under the swamp, under the bedrock. But it comes from somewhere higher."

"Like someplace up in that gully," Lauchie said.

They studied the chamber for a while, noting long streaks of iron deposits that had oxidized to bright orange, making strange patterns on the polished rock. "I want to come back sometime with a string and weight and see how deep it is," Angus said.

"Me, too," Lauchie agreed. "Let's go back and check the first pool again before we freeze."

14

TILT CAVE

On their way back down the tunnel they were able to look around, confident that there were no great holes to fall into. They swung their lights about, noting occasional changes in the rock colors.

"Look at that," Angus said, directing his beam at a bar of water-polished quartz. "It goes somewhere."

Above the quartz, reaching to the roof of the tunnel, another opening branched off toward the west. The entrance was a vertical oval, about two feet high and a little less wide. They had missed it before because they had both been concentrating on the streambed, and because it was angled back from the wall surface.

"It gets a little bigger and seems to slope down and to the right," Lauchie said, shining his light inside.

"Okay, same deal," Angus said. "I go in first."

Here the main tunnel was so low that even though

the branch was near the top, Angus needed only a little jump to pull himself up and slither in.

Lauchie held his light until he saw Angus's wet socks disappear around the corner, and then he set it in the tunnel and followed. The turn was caused by another bar of quartz that ran about ten feet, then the tunnel turned again. The water that had once rushed through had eroded the opposite wall as it turned, making the turn wider and easier. As they progressed, it seemed to mildly slope downward. After five minutes of squirming and crawling, they emerged into a long chamber about twelve feet wide.

"Look at that." Angus pointed with his light. "It's blocked, and we're back at sea level."

At the far end of the chamber was a shallow pool, not unlike ones found on the seashore. There was a slight rising and falling motion to the water, and skiffs of sand were collected in the deeper pockets on the bottom. A rimy ring marked the high-tide line on the smooth stones. The cavern had the same water-washed smooth surface as the rest of the cave, but the far end was more like the blockage at the entrance, made up of huge slabs of strata and smaller broken stone.

"I think this was open to the sea once," Lauchie speculated.

"Still is, in a way," Angus said. "This water is connected to the shore water. It moves with the shore waves."

"Must have caved in once. There could be hundreds of tons covering it." Lauchie lit a candle. The flame bent and softly flickered. "Air, too, filtering through little cracks between the rocks."

"Out in the harbor, all you'd see is the same old boulder slope."

They swung their lights around to the sides and noticed that the old watercourse had cut through the south side of the cave like a streambed, leaving a ten-foot-wide elevated ledge along the north side. It was about four feet higher than the bottom of the cave. Lauchie used a loose stone for a boost and hoisted himself up over the edge while Angus held a light. In a shallow depression, a couple of feet in front of Lauchie was the unmistakable ring of stones that had formed a campfire. When Angus joined him, he was still staring at it in silent wonder.

"Wow. How old?" Angus said.

"Who knows? Four hundred? Four thousand? Before the entrance collapsed."

They slowly began to look about, feeling spooky, finding themselves suddenly speaking in echoing whispers. They wandered around, covering the small area but finding nothing. Even the fireplace was clean.

"I think, maybe, with a high tide and a big on-shore storm, the water might come up over this," Lauchie said.

"Yah. But there would be no waves, just flooding."

They wandered about some more. Lauchie walked along the wall, looking for any kind of mark or sign of human presence. He found a shallow ledge at hip height. It was little more than a crease in the rock, a few inches deep. Sitting on the ledge was a broken arrow tip that had been napped from rose-colored quartz.

"Angus, come here. I found something."

"You always have all the luck."

Lauchie hadn't disturbed it, but Angus scooped up the two pieces to study them. The arrow tip had been split almost in half, in a long diagonal that had left the point with only one notched side.

"It wasn't lost," Lauchie mused. "It was placed here, just the way we found it. I didn't want to touch it."

"Aren't you keepin' it?"

"I was thinking we should leave it right here."

"You're crazy," Angus said. "It's ours—or yours—and it's a real, ancient arrowhead."

"It's ours if we leave it here, in our real, ancient cave, with a real, ancient campfire," Lauchie reasoned.

"Yah. When you think of it like that, it's kind of okay. . . . I guess."

"I wonder what happened to it."

"Maybe it was some young guy on his first hunt."

Lauchie looked around following his light beam. "Yah, I can just see them, maybe five or six guys. They've got a couple of deer, but it starts to rain, or maybe snow."

"So they decide to stay in the cave overnight, keep warm, have a big supper."

"And one of the older guys says to the kid, 'Hey, kid,

hey, Angus, you're supposed to hit the deer, not the rock behind it.'"

"The kid's called Angus?"

"Absolutely," Lauchie said. "Kid's all embarrassed. Everyone laughs."

"His old man says, 'When we get home, you're gonnah have to nap a new arrowhead. Maybe when your fingers are all blistered from napping you'll learn to take better care of your tools.' You think it was like that—like, just the same?"

"Sure," Lauchie said, "different language, different look, but the young guys would get razzed."

"Yah, like first day—'Lauchie, get the lobster gauge.'"

"Gimme a break."

"Well, I think you're right. It's crazy, but I like the idea of leaving it here."

"It's just that he put it there so carefully," Lauchie said. "It's like Ian's shed—yours, too. You know, half the stuff is old, worn-out tools. They're no good, but you can't just throw them away, because they're like old friends."

Angus held his light while Lauchie placed the two pieces of the arrowhead back on the shelf, making it a bit of a ritual. They grinned at each other.

"It's ours," Lauchie said. "This is where we keep it."

"Old Shed Cave."

"In Newfoundland they call sheds 'tilts,'" Lauchie said.

"Okay. Tilt Cave sounds better."

Angus wandered off to explore the cavern.

Lauchie walked over to the old campfire, imagining the small group of hunters sitting about the fire. They would be feeling good because they were in out of the wet and cold and had just enjoyed a big meal. Flames from the fire would flicker on their faces, casting long shadows on the walls. Things said would be remembered at other campfires, and stories would be told about past hunts.

Something about their imagined conversation set Lauchie on another train of thought. It began with the idea of what might have happened centuries ago. Ian had always talked to him that way, teasing and caring, criticizing and teaching. It suddenly occurred to Lauchie that Ian had really looked after that part of his learning and growing up. This wasn't a new idea, but a new appreciation of it.

He had always felt a bit different, as though his father's absence meant that there was something missing, that others knew stuff he didn't. He began to realize that if anything was missing, it made him who he was.

"I don't think there's anything else here," Angus announced. "We should head back. My feet are cold and my socks are trashed."

"Yah. We'll come back another time. I still want to check out that first pool again.

They went and looked at the old arrowhead once more before they left. "It's really beautiful," Lauchie noted, studying its uniform, carefully made edges, each concave nap mark a smooth, tiny, glowing pool of light.

"That's why he couldn't throw it away. I bet he was proud of it," Angus said. "Doesn't feel spooky here anymore."

"I think that's because we thought about how it was—thought about those guys sleeping here, having a good supper together, telling stories, kiddin' around. This is a good place."

As they prepared to leave, Lauchie searched his pockets. He found his lucky red stone that had the shape of a bear. He placed it on the ledge, near the arrowhead—but not too close.

15

GOLD

They crawled into the short return tunnel and soon joined the larger main passageway. Lauchie shone his light at Angus as he emerged from the opening.

"You look like a mouse coming out of a hole in the wall."

"Feel like one, too," Angus said.

"It's nice to be able to almost stand up again, even if it's in ice water."

"Next time we bring rubber boots," Angus said.

They waded in the direction of the stream. Lauchie trailed his hand along the water-smoothed walls of the cave. "When we get to the first pool, we'll start at the outside and work our way in."

"Yah, it's either there or it's gone," Angus reasoned.

At the pool, they separated to opposite sides and began walking in a clockwise spiral. At the very center of the pool Lauchie noticed a skiff of sand no larger than a pie plate. He stooped over and ran his fingers through the sand. There was some depth, and his fingers encountered disklike stones. He pulled one from the sand. "Gold-old-old-old," he yelled, making Angus almost fall in the icy pool.

Angus rushed to Lauchie, making awkward, echoing splashes. "Where? What the . . . "

Lauchie stood shining his light into the palm of his hand. His hand shook, making the flashing gold even more brilliant. Angus bent to rake the sand with his fingers. He stood up holding two more coins. "They're flat," Angus said. "There's no pattern."

"They're worn down," Lauchie said. "Who cares?"

They frantically worked at removing the sand from the ten-inch-deep pothole. Angus held the light and Lauchie raked the sand with his hands, dispersing it in the surrounding pool and handing Angus the coins. It was soon obvious that they had them all. The smooth, round hole was clear of both sand and gold. Lauchie stood up grinning at Angus, who now had the flashlight tucked under his arm, his cupped hands holding the coins.

"It's real," Lauchie almost whispered. "Let's get out of the water."

"This is it!" Angus said. "We're rich!"

"It's gold, real gold!"

They were wafer thin and oval shaped, so worn by the action of the pool that there was no hint that they'd once been coins. The weighty feel of gold was apparent only when several were held together. There was no sign of the silver; perhaps its lighter weight had caused it to be completely worn away. They placed the coins on a flat section of rock and continued to look for more, at first frantically, then more thoroughly, but the fact that the coins had all been found at one place in the pool indicated that the current had probably drawn them there.

Angus stopped moving around the pool. "I'm freezing."

"Yah," Lauchie agreed. "I don't think there's any more. We'll come back soon anyway. Look at the hole. It's starting to refill with sand."

"Hey! We're *rich-ich-ich!*" Angus's voice echoed.

They clambered out, shivering with the cold, laughing and pounding each other on the back. Dimly lit from the peripheral glow of their flashlights, they jumped about, talking over each other, bumping fists.

"We—"

"—did it."

"We d—"

"—id it!"

With the gold splayed on the rock between them, they quickly pulled off their wet socks and put on their dry sneakers. "Freeeezing-ing-ing," Lauchie stammered, struggling in the dark.

"We did it! We did it!" Angus said. "Let me hold them. Wow, feel the weight."

Lauchie added his light to Angus's. The gold glittered magically in Angus's hands. "We're the best!" Lauchie turned his light onto the other pool to find his mark. The long "V" was much higher than the water now. "Look—the tide's going out. I bet at full high tide it rises above the falls and then flushes the pool when it goes out."

"Good thing gold is heavy," Angus said.

"Let's count it." Lauchie held out his cupped hands, with his flashlight tucked under his arm.

Angus dropped the coins, one by one, into Lauchie's hands. "Nineteen, twenty, twenty-one, twenty-two, twenty-three. Wow!"

"Yah," Lauchie said. "Twenty-three *peso grandes!*" He wrapped the coins in a wet sock and put them in the backpack. Deciding to leave the rope there for future explorations, they started back up the slope. They got to the place where they had found the old chest bottom. Angus's light picked up a shape they had missed before. It was caught in a crack in the old boards. Lauchie picked it up and showed Angus. The coin that rested in his palm was dull, black, oxidized silver, heavy and round, with one flat edge. It was one of the pieces of eight.

"This proves that we got what we came for," Angus said.

"Not quite," Lauchie said, showing Angus the flat place. "Somebody made change. Now it's only six bits, or seven bits."

"I wonder what it bought." Angus poked Lauchie. "Hey, are we rich?"

"Don't think so. But the cave and the adventure—that's special."

"And just finding it . . . a few more years and it would have worn away completely."

"Yah. The doc, Anoogwet Wokwis, the campfire guys . . . so much happened here."

"Now Moose, us—it's spooky," Angus said in a slow, low voice.

"Tilt Cave, the old camp site—that's gottah be the best."

They came to the big rock face. Lauchie began to tie the short rope on to their pack while Angus tied the other end around his ankle. They worked partly by touch in the peripheral glow of the lights lying on the floor of the cave. Angus scrambled through the narrow tunnel, pulled the pack through, then hollered, "All clear."

Lauchie felt a faint tremor, followed by a boom that was so deep and low that it was more like a vibration than a sound. "They blew the big rock!" Lauchie yelled through to Angus, then muttered, "I'd like to have seen that."

A small rock fragment hit Lauchie's cheek. He heard the scampering, scuttling sound of others bouncing down the slope below him, and a faint grating noise. He didn't stop to think. He held the flashlight high in his left hand and jumped, landing with a jarring suddenness on the steep incline, fifteen feet below, scraping his knee painfully as he pitched on down the slope. His flashlight survived the fall and lay beside him, casting a golden wedge of light along the floor. Small shards were still pinging down the grade, but it seemed that nothing major had happened and he felt foolish about jumping. His left ankle hurt from the leap and his right knee was bleeding through a tear in his jeans. He shone the light up toward the ledge. The opening wasn't visible from down below, and the light showed only the face of the big obstruction above it.

A few more shards bounced down the slope. The rock face shuddered in the light beam, as though his hand were shaking and causing his light to tremble. Then a great grinding sound escalated to a roar, and a huge section of the face seemed to slip. Lauchie curled himself into a ball at the base of the second wall. He was suddenly hit with a wave of dust so thick that he could feel it. He crouched, feeling the blows of rocks hitting the wall beside him, then scampered around the protective wedge and jumped into the blackness, dropping down to the pool. Here he was safe from rocks.

The light beam was like a dim glow in heavy fog. He moved his hand about him on the floor and discovered the familiar feel of the rope. He gave it an experimental tug. It was free. Some sharp and heavy rock must have severed it.

Angus, he thought. *Are you alive? Is your side safe?*

He pulled the rope in and coiled it in the dark, then felt his way around the apron of the pool and into the south tunnel. Here the air was suddenly clear and fresh. He wiped the dust from the flashlight lens, marveling that it still worked, splashed some icy water on his face and scooped up a drink, then spat grit and had another drink.

"I've got water and air. Every miner in the county will be on that rock face in an hour. They'll be afraid to blast. They'll have to drill and break all the way. My God, I'm talking to myself. . . . if Angus is okay . . . must be . . . on the solid side . . . big rock wedged . . . He's gottah be. I've gottah stay calm. . . . maybe a new way . . . over the rock."

Lauchie waited upstream for the dust to settle. He endured the icy water for five minutes, then ventured back toward the pool. The air was still dusty, but now his light cut through it.

He climbed the slope, this time without the rope. He kept looking up and forward, hoping to see a glimmer of light. There was nothing. At first, the face didn't look much different, but then he saw it. The giant rock had cracked, and the two halves were slightly skewed. The south side had dropped down, filling the ditch and sliding forward until it had once again wedged against the ceiling. At the sides of the cave, new shards of strata littered the floor. There was no easy way out.

He approached the face, stood still, and listened. Nothing. He shouted, even though he knew that no sound would penetrate the wall. The futility of shouting unnerved him.

He decided to head for Tilt Cave, where the air would be good. Angus would be on his way up the rope by now, he thought . . . he hoped.

When Lauchie arrived at Tilt Cave, his light was still strong, but it had occurred to him that he would have to start conserving the batteries. He decided to allow himself about ten minutes exploring the seaward face of the cave more carefully. He had lots of matches and three candles in his pocket. The candles were broken, but the wicks held them together.

He found a place about midway in front of the seaward end, sat down, turned off the light, and waited for his eyes to fully dilate. He scanned back and forth, up and down, looking for the tiniest glimmer of light, which would indicate an opening. In the darkness his mind became a tumult of images and thoughts. He and Angus had always looked out for each other. They got in trouble together, and got out of it together. *I'm counting on Angus,* Lauchie thought, *but what if he's counting on me? What if his side was worse than mine? He got through, and the big slab seemed to come forward, into the cave, but. . . .*

He could see no sign of light. He felt around and found his flashlight and the coil of rope and moved down near the water. He repeated the process of turning off the light and letting his eyes scan the blackness. The pulse of the waves was intense in the dark. He felt it like a pressure on his eardrums that surged and retreated with the waves. He imagined himself trapped here, enduring a horrible lingering death. His skeleton, a cave relic. He saw no light and decided to give himself some candle time.

The candlelight wasn't directed, the way the flash-light was. It was just a comforting little glow. Lauchie promised himself just one-half inch of candle. He watched the tiny flame. Instead of flickering randomly, it seemed to pulse like the feeling in his ears. He listened to the wave pulse and watched the candle. They were synchronized. Whatever airflow was in this cave was not from tiny openings in the rock; it was from the rise and fall of the water. He blew out the candle and turned on his light and went to the end of the old streambed, shining the light down along the face of rock. It was deeper here and the light beam picked up the bottom, but the forward side was only murky water. "What am I thinking?" he muttered to himself.

Lauchie anchored the rope by tying it to a rock, then piling rocks on top of it. It wouldn't be strong enough to pull on, but it would stay in place as a guide. He stood in the pool and reached in under the rock face, wishing that he had a pole. There was nothing. He lay in the water and shone his light in. He saw sides and bottom, but what should have been a wall was a void of diminishing light—nothing.

The water was warmer than the cave stream but not really warm, and he felt that he'd prefer the protection of his clothes. The light would be useless but a small comfort. He put his matches and candles beside the rock pile at the end of the rope and began taking deep breaths. *If there's an opening, I'll allow myself fifteen feet in, then return,* he thought. He coiled the rope in big loose coils and let it float at the entrance; he tied the light to his string and left it on. He grabbed the rope in his left hand, took a deep breath, and pushed himself into the opening.

Lauchie wasn't swimming but hanging on during the in-surge, then shooting forward with the outflow. Every foot forward was either a foot nearer to freedom or a foot further from air. Too soon he began to feel an aching need to breathe and the accompanying terror of trapped suffocation. He was about to turn back when his head emerged from the water into damp blackness.

Lauchie stood up, feeling the flow against his body, and turned his light upward. It was just a small chamber, oxygenated by turbulence. He was in a trapped bubble. His light was beginning to dim, so he turned it off and stood shivering in the dark, trying to decide whether to use this good fortune to return or to continue. He waited in the chest-high water with his eyes open. Silver-gray blotches seemed to float around him. He looked down. One of the blotches appeared to be steady. Was it a glimmer of light? Uncertain, and feeling the encroachment of panic, he decided to give it a try, perhaps five surges more, and then he'd return. He took several deep, shivering breaths, timed the pulse, then ducked down and pushed off.

Underwater he saw only absolute blackness. He was attacked by fears even greater than before. A vision of his father tumbling to the sea floor flashed in his mind like a film clip from his old dream. The out-rush seemed to be dragging him deeper. His lungs burned.

He pushed ahead, realizing that he'd ignored every chance to return and that this was his last.

He sensed a glow ahead, faint, perhaps not even real. He was sucked down and ahead in another rip, sure now that the light was brighter. Lungs raged, arms throbbed, numb and cold. Another surge propelled him ahead. The light grew brighter still, and he braced himself against the back-push, fighting his desire to breathe water. Neon spots swarmed before his eyes. His numb fingers slipped and then held as the current paused, reversed, and spat him out into a sun-rayed sea of brilliant green weed and silver bubbles. *His* bubbles, he realized, as he kicked for the surface, releasing the last of his depleted breath.

Lauchie broke through into air, gulped air, felt air. The hard gold light blinded him. He tried to swim, but his arms were like lead and he floated face-down in the water, rolling to take deep aching breaths. He could feel the sun, warm on his back. He felt the breeze pushing him to the shore close by.

Free of his own terror, he began to worry about Angus. Was he hurt, trapped, or worse? He knew he'd be unable to handle the ropes by himself now, but he could go up there, see what he could see. See if the entrance was the same . . . check the ropes . . .

Lauchie felt the nudge of a rock and realized that he was floating in water only knee deep. He grabbed the rock and pulled himself upright, looking up the boulder-strewn slope.

"You fabulous crazy-fool dog!"

Dog was flying down the impossible slope, half-running, half-falling, his agile feet barely touching the tops of boulders, each bound a gravity-defying feat. He could not possibly stop, and Lauchie ducked down behind the rock as Dog hurtled above him and plunged into the sea.

Lauchie hugged Dog. He felt the aliveness of them both, pulse to pulse, confirming the reality of his survival. He looked up and saw someone on the top of the hill. He first thought that perhaps the person could help. Then Lauchie began to study him; he was jumping around like a maniac, like a goofy Angus who started sliding his way down the steep incline, from boulder to boulder, the pack still on his back.

"Angus," Lauchie murmured. "It's Angus." He waved and pulled himself out of the water. They met on the rocky beach with a great victory hug. Noticing Angus's tear-streaked face, Lauchie felt his own eyes begin to water.

"How did you get here?" Angus said. "It's impossible. How'd you get out? The whole hill was on top of you."

"Swam out . . . from Tilt Cave . . . there's a flooded tunnel."

"Incredible!" Angus shrugged the pack off his shoulder and let it slide down his arm to the ground. He stared hard at Lauchie. "Thought you were dead, Buddy," he said. "Tried to keep it out of my mind. Tried to hope you were just trapped . . . but I thought you were dead."

Lauchie noted the traditional miner's "Buddy" greeting, realizing that they'd earned it. They grabbed shoulders. "We're alive," Lauchie said. "Good to see you, Buddy."

They went back to the water's edge and dunked their reddened faces, both coming up talking at the same time. "Don't you ever tell anyone. . . ." They both stopped their admonitions with dripping grins.

"Look at that," Lauchie said, pointing out to sea.

Angus turned to look, and Lauchie pushed him into the water.

"What's with you?"

"That's for *'Rats'* and 'cause I'm wet and 'cause you thought I was dead but you brought the treasure out with you."

Angus laughed, lurching sideways, his feet slipping on rounded rocks as he climbed ashore. "I was so shook up. I think I put the pack on my back. I climbed up that way."

Lauchie used one small stone as a step and climbed onto a huge flat-topped rock. Dog bounded up to join him, gave a shake, and sat with his nose toward the sea. Lauchie turned and gave Angus a helping hand. "Now we're laughing. Five minutes ago I thought you were dead."

"Me, too," Angus said as they both struggled to pull off wet jeans and shirts. "I still can't believe you got out!"

They wrung out their clothes, spreading them out on the rock behind them, and then sat in their goofy boxer shorts looking out over their harbor.

Lauchie told his story first. "Swimming that tunnel was terrifying—worse than climbing the ropes on the cliff, worse than the cave-in. I wanted air so desperately. . . . Then I saw light. . . . When I hit the surface, it was like the air tore down my throat." Lauchie paused. He could feel the hot sun burning deep into his skin. He could smell Dog's drying fur, and he reached over to ruffle his damp ears. "After that, I started to worry about you again, and then I saw Dog flying down the hill, saw you." Lauchie leaned back, braced by his arms and hands, palm down on the warm rock. He looked up into the clear sky. The depth and the blue were infinite. He looked at Angus. "So what happened to you?"

"Right after I pulled the pack through and gave you the all clear, I felt the blast, same as you. I didn't hear the first sounds that you talked about, but I felt a bit of vibration and the rock seemed to shimmy. Next thing, there's this horrible grinding sound, and then *boom!* the big rock just lurched forward. It threw a big blast of dust back, but it cleared quickly. I think most of it went out the opening, caused some kind of draft. I ran to the rock face. Our little tunnel through was mostly gone, and the part that I could see was wedged solid with big broken rock. I think the whole thing split. Each half would be maybe thirty tons—nothing I could do there. I hollered to you, but I knew no sound was going to get through. I needed to get help."

"I was probably on my way to Tilt Cave by then." Lauchie said.

"Yah." Angus shifted his weight to get comfortable. "Going up the rope, with no one there—that was some scary! I was thinking that if I fell, no one would know what had happened. No one would dig you out. I was worried that you might be hurt in there, maybe dead." Angus looked at Lauchie. "I get up over the cliff and Dog's there. He's going nutso. He knows that it's all gone bad. I start runnin' for the wharf, thinkin' maybe someone might be there. Then Dog started barking and veered off to the west, so I followed him. When I saw you, I couldn't believe it at first . . . but Dog, he wouldn't take off like that . . . it had to be you, and then the sun caught your red hair."

They sat for a moment, watching the sea. Lauchie reached over and stroked Dog's soft fur. He listened to the languid pulse of the late-afternoon waves washing against the rock below them.

"So the only way into the cave now," Angus said, "is under water."

"Yep. Right out there. I left a rope guide and there's lots of clearance. Maybe someday, if we had scuba tanks, we could go back. I'd like to see it again . . . someday."

"Sometimes I wonder," Angus said, "in a bad situation, would I do the right thing?"

"There's a big difference between saying what you'd do and really doin' it."

"Sure," Angus said. "The doin' can cause a lot of sweat, fears, an' tears."

Lauchie looked at Angus. "Now we know."

"We even got the prize," Angus said.

"Moose was right about one thing."

"What's that?" Angus said.

"It was a test."

"Yah, well, I guess you passed it."

"We passed it. I can't believe you climbed over the cliff lip with a pack on your back."

"I was sort of in shock."

"Let's see our treasure in the daylight."

Angus handed Lauchie the bag. Lauchie opened it and found his rolled sock. It was heavy, wet, and cave-cold. He shivered and unrolled it, then gently dumped the contents on top of the rock. The thin flat gold pieces spilled out, shining like suns. The piece of eight was dull and black. They each picked up a coin. Lauchie felt the smooth, worn surface, already warm from the sun.

"It's real," Angus whispered.

Lauchie picked up five more coins. He let them nestle loosely in his palm and gently shook them up and down. "First light in four hundred years."

"Lauchie, we're rich."

"Nah," Lauchie said, rewrapping the coins. "But they've gottah be worth a bit."

"Yah," Angus stood and stretched. "Let's go."

They pulled on their damp jeans and shirts. Lauchie shrugged the pack over his shoulders. They took their time going round the short distance of the shore's curve toward the wharf, leaping from boulder to boulder until they reached the bit of beach that led to the wharf's turnaround and Ian's shed. The boats were all back now, the wharf deserted. It was low tide, but the waves rolled naturally where the big rock had once resisted them. They collected their bikes and started home.

Angus threw his arms in the air, riding with no hands and shouting at the sky, "We found it! We found it!"

Lauchie added a great wolf howl that Dog embellished as he ran in circles between them.

They zigzagged down the road that way, laughing when the rough gravel threatened to dump them. Their damp clothes were streaked with dirt, and they grinned at each other with the joy of their adventure and the great accomplishment of surviving it.

"Feel that sun," Lauchie said. "I never want to stop being in the sun."

"Ah, well, you'll never be much of a miner, then."

"I'm a fisherman, not a miner."

"Lauchie, we found it. It's the most fantastic thing that we've ever done."

"Yah, we did it."

"We kind of owe Moose and Grandmother."

"We've gottah get Moose the skates that we promised, with the profit," Lauchie said. "We could send them care of Grandmother so she's kind of in on it."

"Some good old size elevens, courtesy of Anoogwet Wokwis and Doc."

"I think we should keep the silver coin and sell the gold," Lauchie said.

"Something to show our kids," Angus said, laughing in agreement.

They staggered into Lauchie's kitchen with their arms draped over each other's shoulders like two filthy, sweat-streaked pirates, singing, "Yo, ho, ho and a bottle of rum."

Mary laughed. "You two look like you drank your rum in the sheep shed and fell in the trough."

"Mom, you've gottah invite Dan Angus and Marge and Uncle Ian and Aunt Grace over for cards tonight."

"I don't 'gottah' do anything of the kind," she said. "What have you two been up to? You both look disgusting."

"Can't say," Lauchie answered. "We'll tell all tonight."

"Well, company would be nice. Only my curiosity is letting you get away with this. Shall I tell Marge that you're staying for supper, Angus?"

"Yah!" Lauchie answered for him.

"Then both of you go get showered. Try and find something for Angus to wear, and throw those clothes in the washer. You look like you were rolling in dirt."

"We were," Angus admitted.

"Lauchie, where's your belt, and where are your socks?"

"Uh . . . no problem. I've got my socks, and I put my belt. . . . It's somewhere real safe."

When they came down to eat, Angus looked as funny clean as he had dirty. His arms stuck beyond the sleeves of one of Lauchie's shirts, and the jeans rode well above his ankles.

Everyone sat ready to play cards, looking a bit as if they were part of a charade, which they were. Lauchie and Angus disappeared for a moment and then returned, each in turn laying a worn wafer of gold on the table. Angus put down two more saying, "I'll call that bet and raise you one." Lauchie did the same, and then they let the remainder slide from their hands into the center of the table, adding the piece of eight and the pistol.

"You found it!" Ian exclaimed. "Where?"

"In a cave," Lauchie answered. "And that's as much as we'll ever say."

"Oh, Lauchie," Mary said, giving him a quick hug.

"It sounds dangerous," Marge commented.

"There's no cave round here."

"None that you know of," Angus corrected.

"And the cave talk is for this room only," Lauchie cautioned, looking in particular at Aunt Grace.

"I know, I know," she said. "Can I at least tell about you finding the treasure?"

"You bet," Lauchie told her. "You'll be queen of the phone line for a month. We just don't want a bunch of treasure hunters tearing all over the land."

Ian fluctuated between disbelief and embarrassment that something as intriguing as a cave had escaped his knowledge of the area. He could be appeased only with the assurance that the entrance was tiny and had opened only in recent years.

"We found something else," Lauchie said, looking at Ian and speaking in a quiet slow voice. "'Deep in the cave, sentinels there be, numbered seven, all round the treasure they be; bone fingers pointin'. Watchers they be, caterwaulin' and cringin'. Ghoulies all hoary with eyes rummy and rheumy . . .'"

"Oh, no," Aunt Grace gasped, one hand over her mouth, the other to her heart. "Well, Ian, will you hear what you've taught with your evil stories?"

"You've trained him well, Ian," Mary said.

"Eh, well, I wish he had the Gaelic. So how'd you get rid o' them?"

"We kicked their asses!" Angus yelled.

"Angus, that's wharf talk," Marge complained, but with little vigor.

Lauchie and Angus told a very simplified version of their adventure. They described the cave-in as something that happened after they had gotten out, and the climb down the rope wasn't mentioned. They adamantly refused to tell exactly where the cave was located.

As they told their story, Lauchie realized that it wouldn't float for long. He would soon have to level with both Ian and his mom. It would be personal, he decided as he talked, and at some special time for each person.

The idea of giving Moose a pair of skates was discussed. Dan Angus agreed to look after it right away, saying that the boys could repay him when they sold their gold. Angus immediately dug out the winter catalog from its place under the phone book, and showed his mom exactly the skates and size to order.

"Tell them to include a gift card from Anoogwet Wokwis and Doc," Lauchie said. "Send them to Grandmother, not Moose."

They called Mac at home and told him all about it, with Angus on the kitchen phone and Lauchie on the front-room extension. Mac suggested that the museum buy the gold, paying by weight, and display it with the letter, which no longer needed to be kept secret. He suggested that they come the following Saturday. Mac wanted to chat with Mary, so Angus passed her the phone and took her place at the table.

"Could you take us, Uncle Ian?"

"Ah, well, I suppose we could bait heavy on Friday. Dan Angus and I are neck an' neck for top weight at the wharf. It'd be a clear shame if he got ahead." Ian slowly scanned the table, but got no reaction, even from Dan Angus.

"Ian, will you just say yes, while she's standin' there holdin' the phone?" Aunt Grace demanded.

"Well, yes, then. I was just ponderin'. Ah, well, let's play cards."

Lauchie was now leaning against the kitchen doorjamb. Angus sat at Mary's place, ready to start the card game while she finished with the phone. He looked up at Lauchie and gave the nod, pulling his chin down a bit and to the left, the way Dan Angus would.

Lauchie smiled.

16

LOOSE ENDS

They'd planned to leave for Halifax after the sun was up, but Lauchie had got up at the regular time. He sat at the kitchen table, sipping a cup of tea. The little pile of gold coins sat on the table beside his cup. He ran the coins from hand to hand, realizing that he would never handle them again. Who had used them? Where had they traveled? What had they looked like when they were new? What had they paid for? He got a heavy brown paper bag from the kitchen drawer and put the coins in it, rolling and folding it like an envelope and reinforcing it with heavy tape. The kitchen window darkly reflected his distorted image like a dusky mirror. "Why'd I have to wake up so early?" he grumbled.

He eased open the kitchen door, then the back porch door, and looked across toward Ian's house. A light was on in Ian's kitchen window. Dog greeted Lauchie on the porch with a low, throaty good-morning woof. "Good," Lauchie said. "Ian's up, too. I can go and bug him."

Lauchie quietly returned to the kitchen, put the bag of coins in the small backpack that he'd packed for the trip, dumped and rinsed his cup, turned off the light, and left. He went down his driveway and back up Ian's to avoid the early-morning dew. When he got to Ian's kitchen door, he tapped on the window and walked in. Ian was drinking tea and a second cup sat, freshly steaming, across from him.

"Mornin'."

"Mornin', Ian."

"Saw your light. Thought you might drop by."

Lauchie sat down and pulled the teacup to his place.

"Well, now," Ian said. "Will Angus be up, too, and ready to go, do you suppose?"

"No way."

"Why not, I wonder?"

"Because Angus is cool. He'll set his alarm for just before dawn and sleep till it wakes him."

"So we're not cool, you and me?" Ian asked.

"Different kind of cool maybe." Lauchie sat, listening to the tiny sounds that the old house made.

"Moose called to thank us," Lauchie said after sitting for a few moments. "He got his skates." Lauchie sipped his tea, letting some more time pass. "In the cave . . . there was a part that used to be open to the sea. It's sealed off now, and no one can ever get back. There was an ancient native campsite there. I found a beautiful arrowhead that had been broken. I left it there." Lauchie paused, sipped more tea. "I told Moose about it."

"And did he think that was cool?"

"Yes."

"So you don't think he's a big dumb Indian, anymore?"

"Wasn't me that said that."

"Didn't disagree, either."

"Ah, come on, Ian. We were just kids then."

"Yah, must have been, what? four months ago."

"Okay, okay, I hear ya."

They drank their tea in quiet thought.

"It's brightening," Ian said. "Let's see if we can roust Angus."

They put their cups in the sink and went out into the first soft light. Ian let the truck roll down the lane at a quiet idle, giving it gentle throttle as they turned onto the road, then said, "You're right, though."

Lauchie looked over at Ian in the dim cab. He was looking straight ahead.

"You were just kids then."

By the time they got to Angus's house, he was up, and the sun was cresting the mountain. He came out and walked over to the truck as Ian turned it around.

"I was thinking to take the shore road past the wharf," Ian told Lauchie.

"Good. Angus and I will ride in the back, just until the highway."

"There was a bit of a north wind last night," Ian said. "Lobster will be scarce today."

Lauchie grinned at Ian. He knew that, for some reason, the catch was always poor after a north wind. He also knew that there had been no wind last night. Lauchie jumped out, calling to Angus, "We're riding in back until the highway."

Lauchie and Angus climbed in the back. The truck was still dimpled with dew. Lauchie flipped over an old piece of tarp that was on the truck bed. They sat against the cab wall, on the dry side of the tarp, then wrapped it over their legs, looking backward to the east and the rising sun. Soon they were passing the wharf. The boats were all well out, fishing the farthest grounds first. The sea had a gentle roll, showing a thin streak of white at each crest, and sun flashed off the pitching windshields of the largest boats.

"Our fleet," Angus quipped, watching the boats.

"It's been good to us."

"Yah. I'll miss it when the season ends."

"Moose called," Lauchie said. "He says thanks for the skates. He knows some nice trout pools, way back in, if we want to go camping and fishing after the season."

"Ah, well, I guess!"

"At the campfire—that'd be a good time to tell him all about the caves."

Angus stared out over the sea. "This summer's been the best—the absolute best."

Lauchie pressed his back against the truck's box,

feeling the skittering vibration of loose gravel, listening to the fiddle music drifting from the cab. He watched the gilded corkscrew of their dust unfurl along the cliff's edge; kicked his legs free of the sun-warmed canvas and looked up into the eye-achin' blue.

"Boat ride . . ."